A TEMPERANCE TALE.

Mrs. JULIA (McNAIR) WRIGHT,

Author of "Priest and Nun," "Jug or Not," "The Best Fellow in the World," &c.

PHILADELPHIA:

PORTER & COATES,

Entered according to Act of Congress, in the year 1871, by

PORTER AND COATES,

in the Office of the Librarian of Congress, at Washington.

CONTENTS.

CHAPTER FIRST.

What his Parents did for Him.

"Born of Fortunatus's kin,
Another comes tenderly ushered in
To a prospect all bright and burnished:
No tenant he for life's back slums;
He comes to the world as a gentleman comes
To a lodging ready furnished."

A Million too Much.

CHAPTER FIRST.

What his Parents left him.

TO say that one is born with a silver, or a golden spoon, in one's mouth, has been supposed to assert a rare good fortune. Has anybody ever questioned whether the human being so dowered, may not be most miserably strangled by that beautiful spoon? Even if the victim does not swallow the spoon himself, the nurse may strangle him with it, or some amiable enemy fill it with poison, or admiring friends may hold its shining bowl so near the heir's eyes, that all that is good and grand in nature or in grace may be shut out; and the hopeless prey of a splendid fortune may see nothing but his own distorted image in it.

There are spoons and spoons—to be born with the golden one, is not always to be happy, nor good, nor wise. We are moved to these reflections on spoons in general, by meditating on the history of a youth whose spoon was of the very goldenest.

To begin as early as is possible with our hero—notice him; he is too young for the ceremony of an introduction; but you see first a cambric robe, the length two yards and a half; trimming Valenciennes; tucks thirty-four; moreover you behold a blanket, of which the ground-work is French flannel, but that is hidden by silk embroidery—some poor wretch made it wearily for the trifle of twenty dollars—for she who bought it, although extravagant, was not above making "a bargain" with the seamstress. In the folds of the blanket you may find '*something*' with a soft bald head, a toothless mouth, and a wrinkled red phiz. I give you my word it is a genuine human baby six hours old. The doctor calls it a fine child, and although it resembles the supposed ancestral ape, the nurse is ready to take oath that it is the "finest infant she ever laid eyes on." Being a nurse, her veracity is unimpeachable, and we think of this new baby in the superlative ever after.

This lady in brown silk gown and lace cap who holds the fresh arrival, is Aunt Debby Dean. The tears which have swollen Aunt Debby's eyelids and reddened her thin face are not the gushings of joy which welcomes this heir to the house; they are the agonized outbreaking of a most bitter woe.

This elegant little apartment that will only remind one of a jewel case, so costly and dainty is its fitting up, is the ante-room to that quite royal bed-chamber, whence comes now and then a subdued and very solemn whisper. The door is partly open ; the rich Axminster carpet is scattered with clothing tossed about in haste, and towels dropped here and there; the lace and silken drapery of the bed has been twisted high up out of reach; on the toilette tables bottles are open, or broken or carelessly upset. There is a tread of feet, and oh, they are carrying out 'something,' which but now was 'some one!' Here is a wide board draped in a linen sheet, and a figure stretched out upon it stiff and still; there is another linen covering above this form, and you can see where the face is outlined, and the hands are clasped, and the feet are stiffly placed so near together; the drapery has been pulled aside, here is a mass of black curls falling down, a deadness even now dimming their silken sheen: as they pass along, striving not to jar their burden, a corner of the linen sweeps over the red face of the new-born babe that lies on Aunt

Debby's knee, and there is a quick cry at the strange chill. We hope no more of that mother's mantle, than this one cold corner, fell upon her child: but time will show.

As these bearers go cautiously down stairs, preceded by the nurse, to carry to the grim stately parlors the mistress who now cares not a whit for their splendors, the servant maidens left behind begin to pick up garments and napery, incontinently wiping off their flowing tears on whatever chances to be in hand. Out of the region of their short sobs and ejaculations, walks a thoughtful middle-aged man and stands before Aunt Debby, gazing at the bundle on her lap. It is not the father of this babe—oh no, there has been a double trouble in this gorgeous home. It is the doctor, the family physician, in whose brain our story is now being dimly foreshadowed.

This is not the first time Aunt Debby's tears have fallen; she has had cause to do a deal of weeping in her day, and she strives now to check the expression of her grief. Aunt Debby cannot understand matters. She has not even "a good hope for her dead." She could not possibly tell you whether it is God's will or the Devil's that has just been done. But there is one thing whereof the certainty never falters, she has a living, a loving and a sympathizing Redeemer.

He has been with her in six troubles—he will yet succor in seven ; and though Aunt Debby is no grand saint, though she has done, and, alas ! will do evil in her day, she has a sure refuge in the Saviour of sinners.

"Here is a young heir, Miss Dean," says the doctor.

"Ah yes," sobs Aunt Debby, "and all his great property is not worth to him what parents would be : poor orphaned lamb !"

"He is an heir to more than money."

"Truly, indeed. To immortal life ?" suggests Miss Debby cautiously, as thinking she may be mistaken in her inference, for she knows the physician is not a "church member."

"Well, to that—I hope ; but I had not that in my thoughts. It is my custom to take time by the forelock, and no time is better than to-night to speak my mind to you about this boy."

"I feel that I need your advice, I am sure," says Aunt Debby, upon whose maiden shoulders a terrible responsibility has fallen.

"You are doubtless aware, that traits of character —appetites—sins even—may be hereditary."

"Heaven forbid !" shrieks Aunt Debby.

"But Heaven has not forbidden, has rather ordained ;

and humanity is no loser, for the good can descend as well as the evil; and for the evil, in its indulgence and in fostering it for transmission to our children, we are ourselves to blame, while great virtue and genius are God's gifts."

Aunt Debby felt all at once as if this so costly burden that she was holding, were a coiled serpent, and that she must spring up and cast it away. She reproached herself severely, for in the child's veins ran the only blood akin to hers.

"It might be better," said the doctor, "that this child had been heir to the penury of some sober ditch-digger, than that it had entered into possession of all this magnificence, and with it the taint of parental intemperance."

"Ah, poor dear, how much better for it to die!" wails Aunt Debby, before whom that word Intemperance stands in letters of fire.

"It is not at all likely to die," said the doctor; "the question before it is in what manner it shall live. Over the child's infancy you will have rule. Now, Miss Debby, of all things remember that the one great danger of this child's life will be alcoholic drinks; and you must keep it from them with a vigilance that shall never cease. There is every hope in a correct training: if you begin right and go on right, our baby will end right. You may better expose your little nephew to every contagious disease that stalks abroad, abandon it to the tender mercies of the city charities, or give it for adoption to the pickpocket guild, than waken any slumbering appetite within it, by the use of alcohol!"

"Doctor," replies Aunt Debby with dignity, "you know I would do nothing of the kind."

"An ounce of prevention is worth a pound of cure," retorts the doctor; "and you must not only be circumspect yourself, but you must see to it that others are so."

The body of the dead mother had been laid in state in the parlor; the blaze of the chandeliers had been softened to a pearly twilight; the nurse and the housekeeper began the usual exploration for that mysterious race of cats, who are supposed to haunt the dead, and they then retreated to the hall, carefully closing the doors.

"Mrs. Jillet," said Mrs. Bently the nurse, "I've borne more this day than human nature can survive. I'm completely beat out; and being as our orphan has his aunt to look out for him while I take some refreshment, I quite owe it to myself to do so."

"Ah, you may say so," responded the housekeeper, rejoicing in the prospect of a gossip. "A morsel of cold fowl, a few pickled oysters, and a cup of coffee, may quite set you up, if it is twelve o'clock at night."

"Mrs. Jillet," said Mrs. Bently with pathos, "I must have something even more refreshing than that."

These two excellent women having settled their cap strings and seated themselves in the housekeeper's room, on either side of a table covered with the refection Mrs. Jillet had suggested, the countenance of Mrs. Bently still expressed a morbid dissatisfaction with life.

"Mrs. Bently dear," urged Mrs. Jillet, "*is* there *anything* more I can get to set you up with?"

"I quite owe it to my responsible position," said Mrs. Bently, who it seems had a conscience, "to have a sup of brandy, if there is any in the house."

"*If* there is any in the house!" cried Mrs. Jillet, falling back in her chair and lifting both hands; "if! Why I may say, feeling it right at this solemn hour to tell the truth, that this house is founded, and built up, and walled, and roofed with brandy—and similar. I do not know many things you could ask for here and not get, but I'll take my affidavit if there was one thing missing it wouldn't be brandy," added Mrs. Jillet with some pride, and unlocking a closet in the side of the chimney, she took out a decanter of the precious fluid. Mrs. Bently judiciously added some of this nectar to her coffee, and her face began to brighten.

"I feel that I owe it to our precious orphan to know something of the history of his dear parents," remarked Mrs. Bently, "don't you see it in that light, Mrs. Jillet?"

"I believe it is my duty to tell you what I know, to make you feel at home with the blessed babe, and open your heart to him," quoth Mrs. Jillet. Mrs. Bently hastened to say that 'her heart was open already.'

"You mentioned the brandy," said the housekeeper, "and you bear in mind what I replied to you. Miss Debby's father began life in the liquor business. He had a constitution of iron, every nerve in his body was steel, his heart was as cold as a lump of lead; and I will say for him that he had as much brass in his countenance as ere a man ever I saw." Mrs. Jillet paused and gave a few moments to memories of this metallic individual.

"*Once* he said to me, 'Mrs. Jillet, you're exorbitant on the matter of salary.' He did indeed. As you may suppose, *such* a man didn't drink his own liquor—but he sold and sold, until truly for riches a

Jew is not to be named in comparison of him. When he died and left the money to Mr. Luke Dean, all the son he had, truly he left a pretty sum; and though Mr. Luke put a good deal of the stock down his own throat—made quite a wholesale matter of it—the money has held out, and our orphan's got a million if he's got a penny."

The nurse took more brandy, and the orphan's consequence grew in her esteem.

"Every one do say that Mr. Luke was not his own man for drink, when he shot his brains out three months ago, in the second story front chamber, where you may see marks of it this minute, he then standing at the dressing bureau, and that being the reason Missis had the back room at this present occasion. Yes, Mr. Luke was not in his senses when he did that deed, poor soul—may God forgive him!—A fine figure of a man, and of his property, to put a ball through his head and fall without a cry! I heard that shot, Mrs. Bently, and how I lived I can't tell."

"Neither can I—I'm sure you need a taste to keep your spirits up thinking of it. There, that's right. Now about the mother, my dear?" said the nurse.

"It is not for me ever to say a lady got drunk, and that lady as handsome, and amiable and altogether well dressed, as the Missis; but she took a deal of brandy, wine and similar, for medicine, and sometimes she slept heavy and sometimes was cross, as is not to be wondered at, poor dear—and now she's dead! It's very hard on me, Mrs. Bently."

"So it is—ah! what a dispensation, a mysterious dispensation! And she took a good deal, you say?"

"A deal! ah, oceans of it. After Mr. Luke shot his poor dear brains out, she hardly was herself, what with opium and brandy, having no other comfort. I saw Miss Debby go down on her two knees to her, entreating of her to put it by. More than that, Dr. Roxwell, says he, 'Mrs. Dean, this will be your death, and your child's death. If you go on this way I've no more hope for you than for a dead man. Not one more drop, not one.' He says that a dozen times, if he said it once; but lo, she *could not* heed him, and here's the end. She's gone, just as he said she would; but the babe's safe, thank fortune! Truly, Mrs. Bently, when I laid her out there in the parlor, and thought how he'd gone, and she after him in three months; why, I considered the way she came here just married, three years ago, and they had a wine supper, and everybody toasting and praising; well to mind it just broke my heart! And on the top of that, *you* asking me if we had any brandy in the house—as if we ever were without—it quite cut me.

You may pass me that decanter again, I'll try one more spoonful to warm my bones."

"Oh! I was sure you had it, Mrs. Jillet, it was only a way of asking, you know—me being bashful. But I must go up to our orphan now, poor dear! I will feel it my duty to give up my other engagements, and stay with him these few years, his mother being gone, and his life so important, because of the property."

"Do you that," said Mrs. Jillet cordially: she had discerned in Mrs. Bently a kindred spirit.

We have now learned the family history of this babe which Aunt Debby has faithfully held for some hours. She has not noticed the lapse of time, for she has been reviewing the painful past. Aunt Debby's heart is heavy. Her father—dying Christless; her brother, so much her junior that he seemed to her a darling son, dead by his own crazed act; his beautiful and accomplished wife—quite as surely a suicide, though she would not call her one. Ah! Aunt Debby's beloved dead were not in heaven, and their memories were no benediction. Miss Dean recalled the doctor's caution, and was fully resolved never to permit in the baby a development of its parents' vices. Still, having been brought up in an atmosphere of liquor-drinking and liquor-selling, with every penny in her pocket the result of that lawful traffic, we cannot expect that Aunt Debby had very clear views of what Dr. Roxwell affirmed to be the danger and crime of liquor making, selling, and drinking. In other words, the world called the doctor a fanatic, and Aunt Debby was conservative; still she was determined to have her nephew a moral, sober, gentlemanly, intelligent, and she truly hoped and prayed, a thoroughly religious person.

When next day Mrs. Bently conveyed to the anxious Aunt Debby that it would be quite possible to retain, for a suitable consideration, her services as head nurse for the orphan of the house of Dean—Aunt Debby clutched at that possibility as drowning people grasp at whatever comes nearest the hand. An under nurse, a fine young woman in a gay gown, was engaged to relieve Mrs. Bently in her onerous duties, and Aunt Debby was supposed to be head over all; though this theory was soon proved to be but a pleasing fiction.

Miss Dean having a life interest in the house and its furnishings—indeed she had lived in this home for thirty years—she continued therein unmolested with her servants, the nurses, and the orphan. The parents having died intestate, there were provided, in behalf of the infant Dean and his million, three administrators and two guardians; each of these gentlemen had a legal adviser to instruct him in the duties and liabilities of his position; Miss Debby also retained an attorney, supposed to look after her interests, and to prevent any undue advantage being taken of the heir. The Orphans' Court was expected to see to it that neither administrators, guardians, attorneys, aunt, or babe overreached each other in their anxious care for the million.

It was also evident that the child should have a name. Had he lived "when Rome was," he would have been called Posthumus. To save ourselves the long research and anxious debating that the matter of the name caused Aunt Debby, we will imagine him duly conveyed to church and christened Posthumus Dean, and as this name is so long as to be cumbersome to our pages, we will content ourselves with calling him P. P. is a Problem; he has Property; his life holds Promise; Dr. Roxwell accuses him of having been born with a Predisposition. If guardians, friends, teachers, society, and the laws of the land do an honest part by P., there is no reason why his name shall not stand gloriously high as any on the mighty roll of fame—he will found a church; endow a college; write a book; establish a great business; live a philanthropist and die a Christian. We have great hopes of P. The doctor says he has a tremendous vitality, and we know he is heir of a million.

CHAPTER SECOND.

What the Nurse gave Him.

"Born in wealth, and wealthily nursed;
Capped, napped, papped, and lapped from the first,
On the knees of Prodigality."

CHAPTER SECOND.

What the Nurse gave him.

WHILE many a poor babe gets on during the first months of its life, with no care but that hastily given in odd moments by an over-worked mother, our infant P. was provided with two nurses, and Aunt Debby had serious thoughts of engaging a third. Aunt Debby, with the responsibilities of a baby resting on her soul, was an object of compassion to all right-minded people. She sat in nervous excitement watching Mrs. Bently and her assistant, Ann, wash and array the little heir. At last she spoke her mind. "Mrs. Bently, we must get our baby a wet-nurse."

"Not for the world!" cried Mrs. Bently, who wished no one to dispute her supremacy, or have a right to the services of Ann. "Wet-nurses is dangerous. We can feed the child beautiful. Why it is a true pleasure to see him eat."

"But I've heard that it causes wind on the stomach and colic, to feed a young babe," said Miss Debby.

"Oh that's nothing. Suppose there *is* wind, why

a sup of gin and sugar, with a drop of hot water, will cure the colic immegit; and the child will fatten on it wonderful," replied Mrs. Bently.

"Gin? But Doctor Roxwell don't approve of gin.'

"Don't? well, all the wisdom of the world ain't in doctors. Let me tell you, ma'am, doctors that *do* know recommend gin. I've heard them frequent—besides *I've* had the care of some two hundred infants, and *I* ought to know."

"I want everything done for the best for this child," said Aunt Debby anxiously.

"That's the very reason I say don't get a wet-nurse. I've known children to take the scrofula, or the tatter, or the clipping mania from them kind."

"What's clipping mania?" demanded Ann, alert for information.

"It is picking up things, quick like," explained Mrs. Bently.

"O, some sort of slight of hand," said Ann.

"But, Mrs. Bently," urged Aunt Debby, "you know we might get a person who had no troubles of this kind."

"One never knows the harm that may be in them," said Mrs. Bently sententiously. "Now when you feed a child milk or farina, or cracker water—there it is in the cup before you—you know all about it;

and if it is ailing, a few drops of cordial, a spoon of gin, or a taste of brandy in water, will cure it at once, and that you know is harmless, and will never leave a trace of evil behind. Indeed, ma'am, one can't be too careful of babies."

Aunt Debby yielded to Mrs Bently's superior wisdom; but while some infants get through the little oft-recurring ills of babyhood, physicked only by dame Nature, the small Dean had a medical attendant ever on the watch over him, and that physician was Doctor Roxwell. The doctor unexpectedly appeared in the grand nursery, with a healthy young foster mother in his wake. Our orphan was slumbering in Ann's lap: he was too precious to lie in his cradle in the day-time, so the nursemaid held him while he slept, and Mrs. Bently sat over against her, severely watching to see that she held him properly.

Mrs. Bently was a woman of resources; since she could not prevent the installation of Mrs. Green, she considered that the best thing to do was to cajole Mrs. Green into subservience to her wishes. She therefore welcomed her with effusion, declaring that her arrival "set her heart quite at rest." She also aroused little P., and handed him over to his new attendant, at once, secretly hoping that the child would rebel, and refuse to receive the proffered service. Unfortunately for

Mrs. Bently, the orphan took to his legitimate refreshments with avidity.

Thereafter the nursery at the Dean mansion was a spectacle for mothers. Aunt Debby walked through it once in two hours, looked about, helplessly conscious of her own ignorance, and departed. Each of the three nurses was mortally afraid of doing more for the child than absolutely belonged to her office. They differed on every point concerning this boy—what he should wear, how his three hairs should be brushed, what should be the temperature of his bath—and when, how often and how far, he should be taken out for exercise.

On account of these discussions it not unfrequently happened that the babe's bath was one day very chill, the next day almost scalding; he was supposed to be born with an antipathy to water, because he invariably shrieked when he was getting washed.

Mrs. Green thought P.'s mouth should be rinsed out with clear water; Mrs. Bently thought it should be sherry and water; Ann thought it should not be rinsed at all; all these plans were tried. Amid disputes as to whether nine, one, four, or intermediate hours, were the most suitable for P. to be taken out, about half the days in the week he remained in altogether. When he did go out the procession was a sight to be seen. Little P. had a state coach with gilding and lace, ruffles and satin; a coach for a baby king. In this he was laid, enveloped in a down-bordered cloak, his head covered in a cap and his face smothered under a zephyr veil. Ann in her most radiant chintz went to wheel the coach. Mrs. Green in her new poplin walked alongside lest little Master should get hungry; and Mrs. Bently, grand in black silk dress and shawl, followed after to see that all was right, carrying in her pocket a bottle of cordial, for fear her charge should be attacked with cramp.

When evening came Mrs. Green found it needful for her health that she should go out for exercise, also to visit her aged mother, and her own infant. On these occasions Mrs. Green surreptitiously divided with her own flesh and blood, the nutriment which she had duly sold to our orphan, for part of his million.

While Mrs. Green was thus nefariously absent, Mrs. Bently, "to keep her spirits up," devoted herself to sitting with the housekeeper, where gossip was seasoned with drops of "brandy and similar," to quote Mrs. Jillet.

Ann was thus left with our P.; but this girl's special passion was novel reading. With much secrecy she therefore administered to her nursling certain doses of "Doctor Morbus' Universal Baby Panacea," and while he slept profoundly thereafter, Ann's innocent mind was devoted to the mysteries of "The Robber's Cave," "The Black Bandit," "Death and Danger," and other useful and enlivening works, part of the swarming progeny of a "free press."

When Mrs. Green was introduced to the Dean household, she was a tidy, cheerful, healthy woman, who had lived plainly, worked hard and slept soundly, all her life. To her, ale, beer, porter, and London stout were unknown.

"Indeed you must drink something of the kind, or you'll never be able to nurse our baby," said Mrs. Bently.

"I have always done well by my own children without."

"O, that's different," said Mrs. Bently. "Come now, you must do your duty; and suppose you don't take to the taste, it will come more natural by and by. I'd as soon go without my dinner, as have it without a glass of ale. Some take tea, but I'm weakly, and need what is stronger. It will be very unsocial not to drink with me and Ann."

Thereafter among the bills sent in by our orphan's guardians to the administrators of the estate, on behalf of said orphan's household expenditure, was an item of three bottles of best ale daily, for the nursery table. Under this regime Mrs. Green grew fat and florid. "I told you so," said Mrs. Bently with triumph. "Now you see that ale agrees with you."

Aunt Debby was one of those gentle natures who must have some one to love, and her affections were wrapping themselves about little P. There were many hours when the dear lady planned how she would guide and train her child "when he grew old enough:" she did not know that her training should have commenced with its first shrill cry of greeting to this world. Aunt Debby also did a great deal of praying for her nephew—on her knees she pleaded the case of the orphan; but she failed to watch as well as pray. Not only did Aunt Debby fail to watch, but she had a somnambulistic fashion of not seeing, or realizing the importance of what passed before her eyes.

"What are you giving Baby?" Aunt Debby asked of Ann.

"Just catnip tea, ma'am."

This was harmless truly, but a suspicious odor came up to Aunt Debby's nose. "Seems to me it smells of whiskey."

"Just a little Mrs. Bently put in—she always does it."

"But why? What is it good for? Is he sick?"

"No indeed, ma'am, healthy and well; but this is to keep him so—He's always had it, ma'am, and it is good for—why pretty near everything—I guess."

"O," said Miss Dean, blankly, and went her way, unenlightened, unsatisfied, convinced of her short-comings, but sure, or trying to be sure, that all must be right with a baby who had a doctor and three nurses to take care of it.

Even these guardians could not prevent the child having some sharp twinges over the process of teething. When the heir was roaring or struggling, or worse, lying weakly on Ann's arm, Aunt Debby would sit plaintively sighing, wiping away silent tears, and making feeble suggestions of peppermint. Over some idiosyncrasies of this infant's stomach Dr. Roxwell was greatly puzzled; Ann having never mentioned the little matter of the "Universal Infant Panacea," and Mrs. Bently being ready to take oath that "she ever used the babe accordin' to medical orders," the doctor failed to suspect the real cause of many physical eccentricities.

Aunt Debby was one day solicitously watching a hot bath which the doctor had prescribed for his baby patient. "Is not that something the doctor did not mention?" she asked, as Mrs. Bently gave the water a liberal dash of Bourbon, and proceeded to put the child's flannel bandage to soak in brandy.

"O, there are things any good nurse is expected to do without special orders. Indeed Miss Dean, there is few things about children that whiskey is not good for. Take it all in all, I'd as soon be without flannel or medicine, or water itself, as without a bit of good whiskey for Baby."

Aunt Debby, if neither convinced nor converted by this reasoning, was most effectually silenced.

Under Mrs. Bently's tutelage, Mrs. Green had changed greatly. The bottle of ale at dinner did not quench a thirst which she affirmed arose from nursing the orphan. Of course in these refined modern days no nurse thinks for a moment of having half a glass of brandy and water on rising, ale at noon, and a night-cap in the form of hot toddy. These helps to her exhausted nature Mrs. Green asserted she must have, for the orphan was a ravenous babe "who took all she ate;" if said child also took all she drank, he must have been pretty thoroughly saturated with the particular style of fluids which Dr. Roxwell had prohibited.

As we have hinted, the morning toilette of Master P. was a momentous occasion. Mrs. Bently bathed the baby, because one of the few things on which meek

Aunt Debby insisted, was, that no less skilful fingers than those of the *Head Nurse* should perform this important task: before Mrs. Bently knelt Ann to hold pincushion, powder-box and towels, and to hand over the different garments as they were required: Mrs. Green sat near, lest the infant should get uproarious and demand refreshments after the fashion of juvenile Micawbers. In full view was Aunt Debby, in a dress heavily trimmed with black crape, a deeply bordered kerchief, jet jewelry, and a mourning-cap. At Mrs. Bently's hand might ever be seen a goodly array of bottles. Bottle 1 was best Bourbon, some of which went into the bath, "to make it safe;" bottle 2 was brandy, wherewith P.'s head was rubbed, "to prevent his taking cold, and to make his hair grow;" bottle 3, whiskey of proof, "to rub the infant's back and make it strong;" bottle 4, best Hollands, to make a spoon of toddy for P., "to keep off the danger of colic after bathing." All this was graciously explained to Aunt Debby by Mrs. Bently.

"But really," said Miss Dean, "it seems to me that gin must be injurious to Baby. I should think a child's stomach altogether too delicate for such fiery liquids."

"But it's diluted, ma'am."

"Still it is there, a spoonful of it."

"Well, ma'am," said Mrs. Bently, with the air of a martyr, "these things do look strange to those who do not know much about babies. It needs a person that has had the care of two hundred of them, as I have, ma'am, to know how to raise them right. It is my duty to do my best by this orphan, but if I ain't permitted, why I ain't—that's all. It *may* be, ma'am, as you could find some one who'd suit your idee better." Mrs. Bently spoke as one who greatly doubts, and her hint of departure threw Aunt Debby in despair. "O, to be sure you know best, Mrs. Bently; I would not hinder you from taking any course that is proper for our Baby. I leave it all to you, and his life is so precious, you know—the last of his name, and all this property—the whole family credit depends on him."

"True indeed, ma'am, and as I was telling Mrs. Jillet, we are bringing him up to be a credit. A finer child was never seen. Don't alarm yourself about the sup of good liquor he gets, Miss Dean. Why, there's the little Dutch babies as are just reared on lager and other things of the kind, the finest-looking children ever one saw."

"I'm sure I didn't know those people used beer and liquor for their children more than we do," said Miss Dean.

"Perhaps, ma'am," replied Mrs. Bently with an injured air, "you haven't been to Chicago like as I have. Was sent for there, to nurse a baby, ma'am, and I saw the children, just toddling about, that could drink off their mug of lager, and scream like Injins after it, ma'am; they were so fat they were broad as they were long, and their cheeks had the red on them like red paint. O, I've seen something of babies, I can tell you, ma'am."

About this time Dr. Roxwell began to look suspiciously at Mrs. Green. She had been a favorite of his, because she was an honest, bright, well-tempered woman, with a light step, and a merry smile. She was growing indolent and heavy-eyed; the pink on her cheeks had deepened into purple; her laugh had ceased to ring out clearly as she hugged and tossed her little nursling. The old mother who stayed at home and took care of the two babies that Mrs. Green had left behind her when she went to earn good wages from the hungry heir, had come one evening to Dr. Roxwell.

"Doctor dear, there's something amiss with Jane. She's not herself at all. I'm fearing somebody is leading her off to drink, and indeed I always heard that was an unlucky house for liquor. Sure it's built with the price of souls, and the young couple went a bad way, may the Lord pity them. But look after Jane, doctor dear, for her husband is off to the mines, a rare decent lad, and if she goes a wrong gait she'll break his heart, not to mention me own."

The busy doctor tried to look after Jane. He talked to her, but she denied the whiskey accusation flatly.

"It is the high living and easy work, doctor. I never take a drop, barring a sup of ale when I'm faint, that boy is so hungry, doctor. Sure he eats as if he was worth a million."

The weather was warm and the doctor dared not make a change for Master P., although he accepted Mrs. Green's assertions with qualifications.

Mrs. Green slept in the nursery with P. in a crib by her side, and used to lift the little one into her bed at night. There was a black bruise found one morning on this orphan, which set Aunt Debby nearly wild, and for which no one could account, that is, none but Mrs. Green, who would not say that she had dropped this little unfortunate between the bed and the crib, she having taken an unusually large night-cap just before she took the child. Perhaps it was this mystery that made Aunt Debby restless at night, and careful overmuch, as she thought of this small morsel of humanity, her nephew.

One night in October, the little one being then a

year old, Aunt Debby wandered into the nursery. P. was not in his crib. She glanced to the bed; thence came the sound of long-drawn snores from Mrs. Green, but no baby was visible. Aunt Debby cautiously moved the bed covers, and there only a pair of quivering fat legs could be seen from under the heavy arm and shoulder of the nurse, who had rolled over on our baby. Mrs. Green had come very near ending our history then and there. When Aunt Debby succeeded in prying her off this unfortunate child's head, he was seen to be black in the face, and nearly lifeless.

The little confusion at Babel was nothing to what reigned for the next few hours in the Dean mansion.

Early in the morning Mrs. Green having awakened with a clear conscience, and utter ignorance of the events of the past night, the doctor pronounced the baby weaned, and sent the nurse home in a carriage, with as much good advice as she could carry.

That evening Dr. Roxwell discussed our orphan with his cousin Nancy. Nancy being old was deaf—for ten years no sound had penetrated her tympanum. The doctor liked to talk to her: he had the convenience of soliloquy without its absurdity. Cousin Nancy always looked at him fiercely, nodded her head frequently, and never disputed anything, however wild.

"I wonder if P. is doomed?" said the doctor.

Is his ruin a foregone conclusion, because of his parents' intemperance? If he escapes a hereditary danger, have the measures of his nurses insured his destruction? If he is free of injury from parents and nurses, what is society going to do for him? P. is not at all to blame thus far, he is helpless. Will he ever be to blame however he turns out? If there is in public sentiment or in civil law any power to save him and it fails to be exerted, and he goes to perdition, shall we condemn P. or the power that was not applied?

CHAPTER THIRD.

How Aunt Debby helped Matters.

"You can believe
Sordello foremost in the regal class
Nature has broadly severed from the mass
Of men, and framed for pleasure———"

CHAPTER THIRD.

What Aunt Debby did for him.

BABY P. by a miracle survived the reign of his three nurses. As we have shown, the last achievement of Mrs. Green was to suffocate the Heir of a million.

Aunt Debby put in Mrs. Green's place a silver salver, a silver bowl, and a silver spoon so heavy that the poor Heir found it very difficult to handle.

Mrs. Bently's rule lasted a year and a half after Mrs. Green's departure. The longer she remained the greater privileges she arrogated to herself, and it was not unusual to find the nursery filled with the head nurse's friends, all of whom were getting treated at the expense of the orphan. On one of these occasions Aunt Debby sent for little P. to be brought down to the parlor that she might exhibit him to an admiring acquaintance. Our P. was a fine-looking child, tall and strong. Usually very bright in face and speech, Aunt Debby delighted in his gracious way of receiving his guests, and in the acuteness of his replies. But on this unhappy day all was changed.

The Heir stood with round, wide-open, owlish eyes and a stupid stare; his under lip fell, his forefinger was thrust aimlessly into his throat, he swayed about with his head on one side, and replied to every word with an inane grin.

"Dont be silly, my boy," said Aunt Debby. "Why, how you act! where is our little gentleman? Come, be polite and speak to us."

But it was evident that P. was doing his very best, and that it was bad enough. The child had no control over his staring eyes and drivelling mouth. Aunt Debby gazed in horror. This idol of her soul had become idiotic; it was apparent that he had been allowed to fall, and the jar had ruined his brain. She shrieked to a servant to run for the doctor, and laying her boy on the sofa hung over him, clasping the idle hand that would go into his mouth, and looking tearfully into the round silly eyes, her soul shrinking with horror at the queer "he! he, ha!" the only sound which the usually bright and merry P. seemed capable of producing.

The doctor came with speed, and Aunt Debby met him, wringing her hands, tears streaming over her face.

"O, doctor, our boy is idiotic! My child's brain

is ruined! Oh the bright lovely darling—look at him—he knows nothing at all!"

The doctor carefully examined his little patient, and then without a word went up stairs.

"Can't you help him, doctor? Will he always be this way?" cried Aunt Debby, when the physician again stood by the sofa where P. lay.

"He'll come to himself, Miss Dean. The child is drunk. That fiendish nurse up stairs has been feeding him with whiskey, and her company have let him eat the sugar out of their glasses of brandy and water until he is at the silly stage of drunkenness; and to tell you the truth, Miss Dean, I had as soon have seen him idiotic; this business is much worse than you imagined. I have advised that Bently to leave as soon as possible, and you had better go and enforce that by an order. If she stays much longer here, there will be a Sensation Murder in to-morrow's paper, and I shall become known to fame."

A baby drunk! This gibbering infant idiot was the victim of King Alcohol. Do you wonder that with the memory of that sharp pistol-shot which had heralded the father's self-destruction, with the thought of that young mother's wretched fate, the soul of Aunt Debby grew sick within her, and that gazing on her baby's unmeaning face she entered into the bitter Valley of the Shadow of Death?

"It is possible that the injury to his mind may be permanent," said Dr. Roxwell, "or he may be restored. But look you here, Miss Dean. The use of liquor renders one physically likely to crave it; it opens brain cells that do not close. Now tell me, if you can, will this child ever be held morally accountable for his sins if he becomes a drunkard, or will the parents who poisoned him before his birth, or that wretched woman who has thus imposed on his infant helplessness, be accountable?"

"O, doctor," cried Aunt Debby, smitten with a sudden dread, "will *I* be accountable! I wanted to do what was right, to train him well—and see what he has come to."

"And how far have you trained him, Miss Dean?"

"Already? Why he is too little; I have been waiting for the time to come."

"You have let many precious hours go by," said the doctor.

P. came out of his imbecility. Next day he seemed "as good as new." Mrs. Bently was gone, and the Heir did not appear to miss her greatly. Aunt Debby said that Ann was a kind, well-meaning girl, moreover "young and biddable;" and as Ann was supposed to have gained experience during her tutelage to Mrs. Bently, she was now given full sway over the nursery, with directions not to allow little Master any beer, brandy, or other intoxicating liquors.

On the second day of the new reign the screams of the small lord of the mansion pierced every ear. Miss Dean was receiving morning callers, but as the outcry rose more furious each instant, she was forced to excuse herself, and go to ascertain why so great wrath existed in this celestial mind.

"Deed, ma'am," said Ann, who sat with a flushed face by the nursery-table spread with conventional boiled mutton and rice pudding, "it is just because little Master wants his beer, ma'am, which the doctor said I wasn't to give him."

"That baby cry for beer!" exclaimed the aunt. "Why, the taste of it ought to be odious to him."

"Maybe it ought, but it ain't. No indeed, he likes it far better than milk or water—and me offering of him both."

Our P. had been performing a war dance about the room, whooping madly at intervals. He now pointed an accusing finger at his maid, and stammered, "She had 'um!"

Aunt Debby looked about carefully, and discovered an empty beer-glass hidden under the table.

Ann saw that it was time to defend herself, and she said, "You wouldn't expect me to go without a glass of ale, ma'am, after taking it regular this two years?"

"You must either go without or lose your place," said Aunt Debby, rising to more firmness than she had ever dared assume with the august Bently. "There is nothing of the kind to be used in this nursery, or in the boy's presence."

The impression made on Miss Dean's mind by the doctor's remark that she had lost many precious hours, was deepened by a brief visit from a lady with two children, one a little younger, the other a year older than the infant Millionaire. These children, to Aunt Debby's astonishment, were able to repeat texts and hymns, and reply intelligently to many questions on religious subjects and Scripture history. They spent some time on Sabbath listening to Bible stories, answering questions and learning something new.

"It is really time to begin with P.," said Aunt Debby. "I had no idea such small children could learn anything. He can say his prayers at least after this."

A look of wonder and horror crossed the lady's face, as she found that the glib-tongued P. had not yet been taught to pray. But it was ignorance, not irreligion, on Aunt Debby's part; and that night and every night thereafter for years, Aunt Debby bent over her boy's crib, and had him repeat his prayer.

P. had been attracted by the instructions given to his playmates, and went with them to their mother's knee to learn. The elder baby concluded to turn tutor to his child-host, and carefully taught him that Samson was the strongest man. Next day he tried to show off his pupil's proficiency, and asked P. "who was the strongest man?"

"Ginger!" cried P., who had paid a sly visit to Mrs. Jillet's store-room, and been nearly strangled as the result of his explorations.

Aunt Debby was quite ashamed of her nephew, and began to teach him forthwith.

At five years old you could not find in all the city a finer-looking child than Mr. P. when he took his walks with Ann. He held himself like a king; his large dark eyes, and flowing masses of black hair—just like the curls that had hung about his dead mother's face—challenged universal attention. Ann rejoiced in arraying him in velvet suits, patent-leather boots with red tops, plumed hats, and frills of choice lace. She felt that some of the grandeur of her young charge was reflected upon her. We must also say for Ann that she never unduly restrained the boy, but let him play how, what, and with whom he would, provided he left her to an undisturbed flirtation with her young man.

Miss Debby, being of a mild unsuspicious nature, placed implicit faith in Ann; and when the claims of society took her away from home in an evening, our lady went with an easy mind, believing that her darling was quite secure with his maid.

Though Ann was willing to charge the Heir high wages for her attendance upon him, she did not feel that his claims upon her time and attention were equal to those of her young man. She began to have a penchant for evening walks, finished by an oyster supper, and for going to the theatre to see the performance of the plays, which she had hitherto been content to read by the light of midnight gas.

Ann tried first one way and then another to get our P. to sleep. The "*Universal Baby Panacea*" had failed to be soporific: after a heavy dose P. was as wakeful as ever.

Miss Debby had gone away one evening, and Ann was longing to get off to a dance with her young man. She hit upon the expedient of frightening the boy to sleep. She put him in bed, and sat down to read—her voice was a loud monotone—and she began with "A True Account of one Count Le Roy, who was guilliotined in Paris, and thereafter walked with his

Head in his Hands to the Cemetery of St. Genevieve." Her tones jarred on P.'s nerves; his eyes started with horror; his fat limbs shook under the bed-covers, but no sleep came. Ann kept looking at him impatiently. Her first story ended, she took another, deepening the tragedy of her expression. "The Quarry Murder, being the dying confession of one Wild Walt, who killed eighteen different men."

P. was making various little groans and starts during this reading; he crouched among the pillows, and his black eyes glared about, seeing murderous hands with knives or pistols, in every shadow.

"Why don't you go to sleep, child?" demanded Ann, when this mild tale was concluded.

"O, O, I can't!"

"And why not, do tell—it's long past time!"

"O! I can't, I'm—I'm thirsty." P. scorned to say he was afraid.

Ann wisely concluded that he must be frightened yet further. "Come to the bath-room, and I'll get you a drink," she said; so the trembling child slid out of bed, and in bare feet and little white gown crept with her through the hall, clinging to her dress with all his might.

"I reckon there's ghosts in this house," said Ann, coolly. "There ought to be—a man was killed here once—ah! did you hear anything? I thought I did. Here is your drink."

"Where, where was the man killed?" gasped P., taking a sip of water.

"Why you ain't a bit thirsty—come back to bed with you. Where was he killed? Yonder in the front-room. Ah, don't you see something white? I do. Ah-h-h!"

The wicked girl darted off at full speed, intent only in thoroughly frightening her charge, who sped after her, yelling with terror.

The noise brought up Ann's young man, who waited below. He came cautiously up stairs and looked in. P. was clinging to Ann's neck.

"Can't you get that little fool to sleep? We'll be late. Why don't you give him some laudanum? It is the best thing in the world. Try it," cried the interloper.

"I don't know if there is any, and—I'm afraid of it."

"Pooh! a teaspoonful won't hurt him a hair. Hunt it up and give it to him, I say, or I'll go without you. You are as big a fool as he is. Being up so is what hurts him."

Ann searched the medicine closet for laudanum, and found it; and although some careful druggist had marked it "*Poison*" in red letters, she poured out a spoonful, and not a small one, for poor P., who took it on condition that she would lie on the bed beside him. The poor little fellow crept close to the treacherous creature, and held by her hand until he got into a deep sleep, when Ann at last was able to steal away from him and go to her dance.

Aunt Debby never went to the nursery when she got home late at night; she took it for granted that all was right there. She did not come this night when her nephew's sleep grew deeper and deeper, and the life of the child-heir trembled in the balance. Well perhaps for him, if out of the dread shadow of the coming years he had escaped by some short and easy road to God's peace and rest. People thought he trod a golden path; they envied the boy his wealth; but all behind him lay the blackness of sorrow, shame, and death, and the future hung dark as a winter storm; and what a maze was all the present to this baby's feet! They could not waken P. next morning. His breathing grew fainter and slower still; such a strange pallor fell over his face; and his full lips were purple with a dark circle around them, like that which rimmed his fast-shut eyes. For the errors of nurses One and Two, Dr. Roxwell had been called in haste. He was sent for now by Aunt Debby, who was on the verge of distraction; while Ann, with beautiful candor, was replying to close questions under the heads of beer and brandy:—

"Doctor, is it a fit? is it whiskey again? oh what is it? will he die? our beautiful boy!"

Dr. Roxwell went straight to the point. He looked at the child, at the guilty Ann, and more than guessed what had been done. He spoke fiercely:—

"Girl, tell me how much laudanum you gave this boy! Tell me truly, so that I can save him! Tell me, or I will have you hung for his murder!"

Ann fell on her knees with a cry, and faltered out her agonized confession. "Will he die! will he die!"

"Yes, he will die, I haven't a doubt; it has taken a wonderful hold on him. Die—and *you* killed him."

Poor Ann, she paid dearly for that bad act, for Dr. Roxwell had a patient raving in brain fever at the hospital, long after Master P. was racing about jubilant and strong. Of course the child saw no more of Ann, and Dr. Roxwell, quite in despair of nurses, suggested a nursery governess. The guardians were consulted in due form. They decided that it would not injure P. to learn his letters, and Miss Dean was kindly accorded permission to choose the nursery governess to suit herself. It was one of the compensations such as are ever occurring in this life, that after the direful age of Bently, Green & Co., came a good, pious, loving girl to guide this poor child, who, despite his money, seemed born to misery.

About this time Dr. Roxwell informed his deaf cousin that he had begun to believe in haunted houses and in doomed races, and he thought the Dean home and lineage came in that hapless category—no one that went near them prospered. He said this because he had that morning been called to a little babe, which he found dead. It belonged to Mrs. Green, once P.'s nurse, and the cause of its death was evident to the doctor; the statement was that it had fallen out of bed and been killed by the fall; but Dr. Roxwell was firmly of the opinion that it had been pushed out by the tossings of its drunken mother, and had chilled to death on the bare floor, on that winter night. The doctor shivered as he thought of the little cold creature wailing its life away, its mother too drunk to hear it cry.

Mrs. Green had been travelling a downward path these years. That "decent lad," her husband, looked a heart-broken fellow, and the dollars he had made in mines melted like so many snow-flakes, while his children were neglected, and the old mother on whom the burden of cares fell, grew grayer and more wrinkled every day. She came to the doctor with a piteous appeal. "Can't you do something for our Jane, sir? Ah, it was you got her yon drinking place, bad luck to the day and hour, though you meant no harm, sir, but kindness all. True, then, heaven has no bed for the like of the head nurse who tempted my girl off to drink, and it is only a ruin of a home is left us; and you know she's a soul, doctor dear, and what'll become of that if she goes on?"

"I might help her some if she would help herself. If she really wants to leave off drinking, perhaps I could make it easier for her."

"Willin' is it? Sure she's *not* willin'. And wants, do you say—why doctor, dear, she wants nothing but drink. Oh, why ever did I let her go to that house, where the curse of the Lord lies heavy for the blood and tears and broken hearts and ruined souls that it made in making money!"

The doctor had to hear many plaints like this from the old mother, and some terse, sharp words from the miserable husband, who one day would ask if he might not put his wife in the Insane Asylum, and another would grimly threaten to kill himself and be out of his woe.

"I wish," said the doctor to his deaf cousin, "that I had never seen the Dean house or any one belonging to it! Yet after all I like and pity Miss Debby;

and I think that boy is one of the most winning and beautiful creatures that ever God made."

On Sabbath this child, whom the doctor so much admired, was left in the morning with his governess, in the afternoon with his aunt. The governess found her pupil a "rich and respectable" heathen. Aunt Debby's teachings had not been of a style to take hold of his youthful mind. Miss Gale tried a new system; she procured books of pictures and Bible stories, cards whereon were texts in such beautiful letters that it was quite a pleasure to learn them; and more than all, she could sing; and, instead of Ann's wild love-songs, the nursery now rang to the notes of those sweet hymns of childhood, which Christian mothers have loved and sung these many years. To Aunt Debby's surprise, P. also began to go to church, and to behave quite well during service; this Aunt Debby considered the most remarkable thing she had ever heard of; her nephew being *only* five years old.

CHAPTER FOURTH.

Other Assistance.

"His childhood was one eternal round
Of the game of going on Tickler's ground,
Picking up gold in reality."

CHAPTER FOURTH.

Culinary and Literary Assistance.

IT was a great satisfaction to Aunt Debby that her boy "took kindly" to his letters. He conceived an affection for the alphabet at first sight; his exploits in spelling b-a ba, and b-o bo, were the admiration of the household, and neither pains nor payments were spared. Aunt Debby unfortunately knew no better way of rewarding her little nephew's precocity of intellect, than by pampering his appetite.

We all know the story of the "Three Boys and their Three Cakes." Miss Dean followed the example of the model mothers in that entertaining narrative; and when P. achieved a scraggy A on his slate, or advanced to another syllable in his spelling, she at once repaired to Mrs. Jillet and proposed some eatable as his recompense.

Since P. concluded his first year, he had been giving birthday parties; or at least his aunt gave them for him. Mrs. Bently inaugurated this custom, in order that she might have a grand gossip and supper, with all the stylish nurses in the vicinity. The nurse had said that a child with P.'s expectations could not begin too early to learn to exercise an elegant hospitality; and the strength of custom was on her side; for, as Aunt Debby knew, fashionable little children had parties; and our aunt was one of those women who are always following precedents, doing as others do, and so saving themselves the trouble of thinking.

Miss Gale, the governess, did not feel at liberty to give Miss Dean advice, and was obliged to be silent over what she considered the enormities of the juvenile party.

Aunt Debby said she did not wish to be over-fashionable in her party. She knew that children ought to keep early hours; late eating was bad for their tender constitutions. P.'s guests, therefore, on his fifth birthday, came at six, supped at eight, and went home under convoy of nurses or big brothers, at ten o'clock.

When these thirty children sat down to the table they were a wonderful company; the eyes that should have been fast shut in sleep, were gazing greedily at dishes piled high with nuts and fruit; at plates and baskets of rich cakes of all kinds; at bright clear wine, and brandy jellies; at birds and patés, and culinary nonsense of all kinds. The little girls wore rings and bracelets, necklaces and pins, shining silk and white puffings of lace; and the little boys were all velvet and glitter, and one while they imitated grown people, and talked nonsense about the food and the clothes, and then forgot themselves, and fell in tiffs and rages, and smacked each other's pretty little countenances with their teaspoons, and pulled each other's hair, then went to sobbing and sulking, were carried away, coaxed and comforted, and brought back restored.

When all had eaten to repletion, and lolled back in their chairs, balancing their knives on the teacups, playing tattoos with their forks, and looking generally puffy and distressed, having taken too much lobster and chicken salad, and too many oysters; the butler put by every plate a tiny glass, and half filled it with wine. The small master of the feast was not unversed in wines; he knew what he liked, and just now "golden sherry" was his favorite, so that was the wine given. When all were served, Master P. clambered to a standing in his chair of state, and in a manner carefully inculcated by the butler, and in a form of speech originated by that potentate, drank the health and happiness of his young friends. The little images drank their wine with zest, though there was some hard winking to keep back the tears; and then the glasses were half filled again, and a six-year-old gentleman who had been drilled for the occasion, stood up to propose the health of Master P. and many happy returns of the birthday.

The young orator was confused by so many listeners, and failed in his speech; his sister, interfering with the *mal apropos* criticism common to sisters, cried, "*Happy* Geordie, *happy;* you said *un*happy." "No, I didn't thay it, Thusy," lisped Geordie; and all his little friends giggled at his embarrassment, crying, "You did, you did!"

"I don't care," cried Geordie, goaded to wrath; "I don't care if he has any more of 'em or not!"

"Oh, yes, we do; he has such nice parties!" shouted the children; for already poor P. was followed for the loaves and the fishes—for the gleanings of his million, and not for himself.

Aunt Debby came to the rescue, and drank her nephew's health, so the children got their other half-glass of wine.

After supper, Aunt Debby tried to have them play "blindman's-buff," but they were too full and too cross. Three or four of the wee things could dance, and Miss Gale played tunes for them, in the midst of which entertainment the master of the festivity was found sobbing behind a sofa in a truly deplorable manner.

"What is the matter, my darling?" cried Aunt Debby. When the cause was made apparent, it proved to be that P. could not dance; he was in agonies of envy and—indigestion.

"Indeed, Miss Gale, this is a great oversight," said Aunt Debby; "we will have the dancing-master come and teach him. Don't cry, my dear, you can dance your next birthday."

Miss Gale had a wakeful night. Her charge was restless and feverish; he had ill dreams; suffered with nightmare; talked nonsense; and shrieked in his sleep. Next morning, his head ached; of course he had no appetite, and could not get up. Miss Gale had had time for meditation; she went down to a late breakfast with Miss Dean, and ventured to suggest that children's parties were unhealthful—were likely to make the little ones bilious and dyspeptic.

"They *do* seem injurious," said Miss Dean; "but then other people have them, mothers who ought to know what is right; and I can't be hard on our boy. He will not have another for a year."

"But he will go to several. If he averages one a month during the year, and each one has this effect, I should think he would become a sickly child. Then,

Miss Dean, these parties are bad for the temper. The children get wildly excited, and you saw how cross they were."

"Yes," said Aunt Debby, tranquilly; "I was sorry anything happened to vex my child. We must have him taught to dance, and then he will enjoy it next year."

"And, ma'am," insisted Miss Gale, "I think the parties are bad for the morals of the children. See how envious they are of each other's appearance or accomplishments—how jealous and covetous. The parties foster hate and spite, instead of love; and don't you think it wrong to give children wine?"

"O, yes," said Miss Dean. "I never wish it to be given to our boy. The doctor forbids it. But a glass of sherry once a year for his birthday, is another matter; isn't it?"

"But if that is repeated a dozen times a year at the parties of other little friends, are not the habit and the love of wine likely to be fostered?"

"Dear, dear, I'm afraid so indeed," said Miss Dean.

"And the sherry was not the only thing to cultivate that taste. Those peaches were strong of brandy; and there were three kinds of wine-jelly on the table. I know very few think as I do; but safe side is best side, and I should advocate giving children milk to drink, plain food to eat, childish plays, and early hours; they would be happier and better for it."

"It is a very perplexing question. What can I do?" sighed Aunt Debby.

"Find out your duty, and go straight on and do it."

"Oh, yes; but what *is* duty, and what would folks say? and ought I to set myself up against the customs and opinions of my friends? It is very trying for an inexperienced woman like me to have a child to rear. I really *do* want to know my duty, and I hope to be able to do it. Miss Gale, when you go out to-day, *would* you be kind enough to engage a *very* respectable dancing-master to come here and give that dear child lessons?"

Are we surprised at Aunt Debby? We must consider that hers had been no religious education; the influence of her family had been all for worldliness; she knew literally nothing of any other earthly life than the one she led among wealthy friends, who bounded all their expectations with this earthly horizon.

Aunt Debby had found a something better, loftier, than these associates; but she had no idea of living up to the full extent of her duties and privileges as a child of God. Indeed, she was ignorant alike of duty and privilege. There were many who had as high fortune and position as Miss Dean, in that her native city, who were children of the light, walking in the blessing and beauty of their eternal home; but they were not likely to come within the circle where the rich liquor-dealer's family moved. The paternal business brought its curse in many ways to Miss Debby, and here was one of them; under its doleful shadow she groped painfully along toward heaven, learning the lessons of God's providence very slowly and stupidly, seeing hitherto with half-enlightened eyes, as did he who saw men as trees walking.

And now this woman, who had no fixed principles to guide herself, no steadfast views of duty, no keen discrimination between right and wrong, had put into her hands the training of a child—of a child unhelped by prayerful strivings of a godly parentage, poor offspring of parents who had committed a double suicide, and who now stood dizzily balanced between safety and destruction; great good possible, great ruin probable; he could be saved by some strong guardianship of parents, teachers, nurses, friends, society, law, and they seemed likely to fail him one and all.

As for money, P. was like the heiress of the house of Kilmansegg,

"Gold, and gold, and gold without end;
He had gold to lay by and gold to spend,
Gold to give, and gold to lend,"

and the worst of it was that he was kept fully informed of his golden virtues and prospects, and was taught to greatly plume himself thereon. The coachman blessed him as the owner of the horses, and told him what they were worth a span; the butler displayed the family silver, and told him no one else could claim an ounce of it; the books in the nursery wiled him with tales of the good boy who was very rich and scattered his money by handfuls among poor children who were insufficiently grateful.

As Aunt Debby sent for the dancing-master because other children danced, and gave parties for her boy because other boys had them, so she lavished toys without number, and pocket-money in abundance, on her child. To get a toy, to delight in it one hour, weary of it the next, and make it the subject of scientific experiments the third, was an every-day affair. Miss Gale saw the nursery floor and tables covered with the *debris* of playthings on which had been spent sums that would have been fortunes to many a famished mother whose life was one long "Song of the Shirt," or to bareboned, scarecrow babies turned adrift to pick up their own living among the city scavengers.

"Miss Dean," remonstrated the governess, "I think so many toys, and liberty to break them up, will make him wasteful and extravagant. Would it not be well to limit him, and give him some responsibility about the use of what he has?"

"O, I could not limit the dear boy. It would seem like sheer robbery, keeping him out of his own."

"Still, I think he ought to be taught self-restraint and self-denial," urged Miss Gale.

"That sounds so cruel," said Aunt Debby. "He will have trouble enough, and be denied enough, when he grows up. Let him have everything he wants now."

And so our hero was prepared for the stern reality of life by being indulged and pampered and made the veriest little Sybarite in the land.

Had Miss Gale been wise enough to suggest to Aunt Debby that God, whose love is highest of all, and perfect in all its exercise, does not train his children for their warfare and their crown by yielding to their every desire and fostering their every whim; if she had shown her how to take the dealings of the heavenly love as the pattern of her culture of her child, she might have made many dark things clear, and many crooked places straight. Miss Gale did not thus know how to take up her parable; she could only suggest facts, or state her theories, and Miss Dean, replying vaguely, went on in the old way.

If P. had by any chance objected to his lessons, he might have been permitted to grow up a dunce; but, from some innate affinity with books, or because his teacher had the rare art of making study fascinating, P. kept steadily at his appointed tasks, and during them, enjoyed the—to him—exceptional luxury of being thoroughly well kept in order, and having some one to obey.

Outside of the short daily sojourn in the school-room, life was to the boy a chaos. He was flattered, coaxed, indulged. If his appetite failed, the house-hold stores were ransacked for some dainty to lure his wayward palate. If one game ceased to be amusing, all the world must invent another; when one toy was destroyed, others sprang up in the fashion of the phœnix, each invariably better than its predecessor.

"For a child so pampered," sighed Miss Gale, "I can see nothing future but the misery of disappointment. The poor wretch will have worn out life by the time he is twenty. Pleasure will have palled, only dissipation will be left him, and then death."

Being less philosophic, Miss Dean had none of these foreshadowings; she had supposed that money was ever a blessing for which God was to be thanked, without considering that whether money is a curse or a blessing depends on how it is applied.

Still, in view of the fact that Master Dean is at the mercy of administrators and guardians (of their own interest), we need not be greatly fearful that he shall, on attaining his majority, have the temptation of the possession of great wealth.

As Doctor Roxwell was very frequently called in to rescue our boy from the dangers consequent upon over-eating, and as he piloted the young man safely through the perils of measles, whooping-cough, and other evils that pursue unsuspecting youth, he of course came to understand the heir pretty thoroughly, and concluded that he was a boy who would be good if he could, and would have practised virtue if he had had any encouragement to do so.

"The fact is," said Doctor Roxwell to his cousin Nancy, "if that boy had been born to honest poverty, he has a spirit in him that would rise to conquer obstacles, and he would work his way through the world like a man. Trying to make a useful citizen of him in the way Miss Dean is taking, is like endeavoring to train an athlete by wrapping him up in velvets, feeding him on sweetmeats, and putting him to sleep in down in a room shut up to otto of roses and other disguises of impure air. The question is,

What is responsibility, and who is responsible? and can that boy be anything great or good with everybody so amiably working against him? The best thing that could happen to him would be to be stolen by a gipsey."

Here the doctor's deaf cousin nodded vehemently at the right moment.

During these early years P., having exhausted every pleasure of his existence, resolved on a treat quite new, and in the course of a walk with Mrs. Jillet, insisted on stopping to have his boots polished in the street, by a bootblack. The boy he beckoned to do this service was of his own age, a sturdy tatterdemalion, with streaks of French blacking over his keen countenance. P. put his well-covered foot on the lad's box, and down on his knees fell the child who was born to laborious independence, chuckling as he rubbed and brushed, at the ornate dress and lofty airs of "the little swell."

The two were foster-brothers; this kneeling shoeblack was the whilom babe who had secretly shared with P. the abundance of the maternal fount, during Mrs. Green's evenings out. If it had not been for P.'s pecuniary ability to hire nurses and furnish them with ale, beer, and brandy, Master Green in clean and well-mended corduroys might now have been going daily to the common school; he surely would not have had cause to blush for the maudlin female who staggered up, with, he thought, designs on his earnings, and he held one pocket tight shut while he rubbed P.'s left boot, and was prepared to fight or fly, as the case might demand. It was not Teddy Green who filled the drunken creature's eye just then. She seized her old crony, the elegant Mrs. Jillet, by the hand, and cried, "Come now, it is long since you and I had a treat together; let's go in yonder, and I'll stand a glass of gin each, if Teddy 'll lend me the money; or maybe the child I nursed like a mother will give me a shilling for old days' sake, forby he don't remember them;" and she clasped the disgusted young gentleman in her grimy, foul-smelling arms.

CHAPTER FIFTH.

How his Friends helped Him on.

"I have lived so long I am weary of living;
I wish I were dead, and my sins forgiven;
Then I'd be sure I'd go to Heaven——"

CHAPTER FIFTH.

His Friends lend a Hand.

MRS. BENTLY felt that she owed it to her friendship to Mrs. Jillet to pay occasional visits to the housekeeper, and in doing so, she was careful to choose such times as were not likely to throw her in Miss Dean's way. "I must say," said Mrs. Bently to Mrs. Jillet, "as I don't feel able to meet that lady in friendship. It showed very little consideration for *my* feelings, and very little care for that BLESSED ORPHAN, to break up our agreement all of a sudden so, just because of a little accident. Well, I lay it to Dr. Roxwell, a man as is not the least a gentleman. Do you know, Mrs. Jillet dear, I saw him stop in the street the other day, and have that miserable Green—our wet-nurse, you know—put in his own carriage and sent home, she being too drunk to walk. I don't call that the act of a gentleman as has a proper opinion of hisself."

"Well, indeed!" cried Mrs. Jillet, passing the cake and wine, which greatly endeared her to Mrs.

Bently. "Do you know, she stopped me and young master in the street the other day, and he being the most pertinacious child I ever set eyes on, it took me all the way home making up tales of her being crazy, to put him off."

"For my part," said Mrs. Bently, "I've no patience with people who go on as she does. When you and I first asked her in here to a refreshment with us, she was as innocent as a milkmaid, and had never tasted a thing stronger than a drop of tea, and now she's in the gutter, or the station-house, half the time off and on. I did hear that they'd got her reformed once or twice, but she didn't stay so. I'm quite disgusted with her. I never look at her if I meet her; and don't you do it, Mrs. Jillet; we've nothing to do with that sort, thank fortune!"

"Not I, truly," said Mrs. Jillet, proudly. "Here I've lived this twenty years—and a gentleman's housekeeper is no poor body, let me tell you. I'll have nothing to do with her. It is quite enough I treated her to toddy and egg-nog time and again. There's some people will go on from bad to worse. The butler's coming in after a bit with some brandy and honey mixed, would make one's mouth water." "Very good," replied Mrs. Bently, settling herself complacently. "I've a good boarding-place, Mrs. Jillet, I can recommend it to you, anytime you happen to get out of service." This with secret malice.

"That's not likely," said Mrs. J., tartly. "They can't do without me."

"So *I* thought," said Mrs. Bently. "And you see how it was, and so it will be with you, my dear."

"Not a bit of it. That young gentleman rules here, and I know how to get on with him. He gets a deal here he don't get elsewhere. Wasn't it last Saturday I let him in to suck a julep through a straw, and that pleases every child. The governess is a bit strict with him, and his aunt overmild; for he's a stirring lad, ever after something new, and he finds that something in here."

Yes; Mrs. Jillet knew how to charm her young master. She took him to the circus, and to the rope-dancers, under oath of strict secrecy, and that even surpassed the fascination of the occasion when he had the organ-grinder and the monkey up in the play-room for an hour, and wound out tunes for himself. After that, P. sometimes cursed his stars, with good reason, because he had not been born an organ-grinder.

Though Mrs. Jillet supposed that her fabrications on the subject of Mrs. Green had satisfied Master Dean's inquiring mind, they had by no means done so. He detailed the circumstances to Miss Gale, who seized the opportunity to give him his nurse's history, and make her story the text of a small lecture on temperance. After some searching, they one day found Teddy Green, and had him follow them to the gate of a public square, where he polished P.'s boots and answered questions.

"I stays home when mum ain't taking on too bad. Grannie says it's all along of going to your house, and I wishes she hadn't gone. Yes; pop and me has ruyther a bad time. The big un, older nor me, he's bound to the grocer, and he gets on pretty good. Then the little un, he's dead, and it's good luck for him, only pap an' me cried 'cause he froze, you know, an' freezing's hard on a baby. Not so bad as growin' up drunken, grannie says, and likely 'taint."

"But who takes care of you?" asked P., with wide-open eyes.

"Take care of myself," said the bootblack, coolly.

"And don't you have any one make you wash every day, and get up, and go to bed, and take you out, and buy you things, and teach you things, and always afraid you'll break your neck or get run over?"

"Pooh, no!" said Teddy. "Pop buys me some clothes winters, and I have a rare time keeping mum from selling of them. But I'll be bigger after awhile, and then mum won't boss me, and I'll go to night-school. Black your boots agin some day? Oh, my eye, that's a quarter, and I can keep it all. Now I'll have a sausage for dinner!"

Teddy being gone, our boy was melancholy because his lot in life was not that of a bootblack. But he was growing fast, and one of his guardians purchased a pony for him, and another had him taught to swim; and the butler told him there was an art called fishing, which he might exercise in country places in the summer.

Aside from these new pleasures, there was a high art called Patronage, which P.'s story-books taught him was the part for rich boys to exercise toward small ragamuffins, found lying about loose in the streets; and P. thought it would be grand indeed to take Teddy Green into his royal favor. That was before the palmy days of newsboys and bootblacks; the good times of the present, when they have lodging-houses, friends, and teachers, and not only lay up money for themselves in the bank, but are become rather a fashionable charity.

At first P. contented himself with giving Teddy money, which the recipient at once laid out in provisions for a good supper for himself, father, and grandmother, remarking to P., "What we eats we has, you see; but what we keeps, mum gets, and buys gin; so it's no use laying up, or trying for clothes."

Miss Gale's interest in the Green family grew with two or three visits she paid them. It was so sad to see that poor old mother taking up again the burdens of life, and toiling under them, at eighty years, while tears returned to eyes that had long ago worn out the power of weeping; and, with quick-coming sobs, she bemoaned her daughter's fate.

"Only to think it!" she said to Miss Gale; "the Deans grow rich on the whiskey that ruins my poor girl body and soul! Then there's the law, bless you! they fine her, and she being too poor to pay, goes to jail, and perhaps to the House of Correction; but they can't knock the love of drink out of her. They'd better fine the Deans, and the like of them, that grow rich on it, and these high and lofty ones that sets the poor such a bad example. The law had better be for stopping the sale—that's what it had, miss. The way they do now is just shutting the pasture-gate after the cow's strayed, and sending for the doctor after the man he's dead."

"Come, now, keep your courage up," said Miss Gale, "and you and I will try and save your daughter."

"That's a good word; but hope is clean gone. She is so full of drink all the time, that there's no getting her to try against it. She used to take spells of doing better; but, after what happened the poor baby, I think she drinks to drown thought"

There might have been no hope for Mrs. Green, had not the Dean carriage, one day, providentially run the poor creature down at a street crossing, and broken her leg. The coachman had been trying some of the butler's brandy and honey, and had reached a mental stage when all the world seemed created simply for himself and his horses. Miss Dean and Miss Gale were in the carriage, and the governess saw that here was the hour of opportunity for helping Mrs. Green, and making Miss Debby do something to repair the wrong wrought in her house. It did not occur to Miss Gale that the nurse had changed so that the lady failed to recognise her, and that Miss Dean was personally unknown to the family. They had the injured woman put in the carriage and taken to her home, and, when she had been carried in, sent the coachman for Dr. Roxwell. The old mother kept the poor place tidy; and, when her child had been laid on the one bed, she handed two backless chairs to her guests, and, while striving to undress the sufferer, went on bemoaning: "Here's more trouble along of rich folks. Rich folks is our ruin. If they'd a let us alone we'd done well enough; we're first poisoned, and then killed by them—that we are."

Miss Gale was quietly helping her at the bed, and Aunt Debby exclaimed, uneasily, "Why, my good woman, you look as if you needed some rich person to help you here."

"There'd be no need of their helping, if they had not first hindered. My girl would not have been knocked down if she had not been drunk. But how did she get drunk? All along of rich people, ma'am. She went out nursing a baby, she being nigh as innocent as a baby, and to the full as sober. Well, ma'am, they made a drunkard of her, and turned her out like a dog, blaming her too, ma'am, when they ought to have blamed theirselves. Well, alack! it is a house made up on the price of souls; and, mark my words, ma'am, the Lord's curse will fall on it heavy enough, for we're not the only ones ruined by them. If the making of each of their dollars was the ruin of a soul, they'd have a million to answer for. Their name is Dean, ma'am."

Miss Gale had been plucking at the woman's sleeve to try and check the current of her speech, and now cried, "Hush! oh, hush!" But Aunt Debby rose in dismay. "Dean! Dean! Why, who is this?"

"It's Margaret Green, ma'am; belike you never heard of her. There was two women, named Jillet and Bently, who fair forced the liquor down her throat, and coaxed her on to drink and drink; and, having ruined her, they scorn her now, and call the police if she speaks to them in the streets, forby they often sat hobnobbing with her in other days. Well, the Lord will judge 'em all; and now she's ready, I wish the doctor'd come. I little thought to see her lie like this, without even the change of a clean bed-gown to put on her."

"Green! Green! Why, she nursed *my* boy, and nearly killed him, too. I remember, she *did* change very much in my house; but I had nothing to do in helping her to change."

"Belike, ma'am," said the old woman, drily, "you had nothing to do with *hindering* it. And the Lord often holds us as guilty for not doing good as for doing evil."

Tears swelled in Miss Dean's eyes. "I never thought of this. I was shocked at her nearly killing my poor baby." "She quite killed her own, ma'am," interposed the woman.

"And I did not know she got the habit at my house. O, I cannot tell you how I feel about this; but we will do everything we can for her now. Will we not, Miss Gale?"

"It goes agin me to take your help," said the mother, stiffly; "but we are sore in need."

"And perhaps this will begin a reformation," said Miss Gale.

"I doubt if she *can* reform, she takes so much, ma'am."

"How much a day?" asked Miss Dean.

The old woman held up a quart bottle, which she had found among her child's clothes. "This full, ma'am."

"All that!" cried the ladies in a breath.

"Ay, all that. And she went to *your* house without knowing the taste of it. She learned to love it in your house, ma'am. She came away a common drunkard. Mayhap you know the verse, 'Woe unto him that giveth his neighbor drink, that putteth thy bottle to him, and maketh him drunken also.' And there's another, ma'am, 'Woe to him that coveteth an evil covetousness to his house, that he may set his nest on high. Woe to him that buildeth a town by blood.' Ah, there's a very many of them, ma'am; I've read them time and again, and they're all true, every one."

She stood like a weird old prophetess, one skinny,

brown hand lifted, the other clutching at the shoulder of her daughter, who writhed and groaned on the bed, while, before her, mild-faced, richly-dressed Miss Debby seemed to shrink away from her denunciations.

When the doctor came, the two ladies went home to send stores of clothes, food, and bedding to Mrs. Green; indeed Miss Gale did more, for she thought here was her chance for gaining influence for good over that poor sinner, and so returned to watch with her and care for her all night.

Miss Debby cried nearly all the way home. "She seems to think it my fault," she sighed. "But how can she? I never gave her a drop. I never take any myself, except wine for my dinner; and those jellies and other things are not my fault; cook makes them, and I cannot interfere. Miss Gale, *do* you think I am to blame?"

"Dear madam," replied the governess, "I do not wish to be harsh, but it seems to me that, as God has set you over a large household, you are responsible for what is done under your roof. You should absolutely know what is going on, and forbid and prevent evil. I should say you *could* interfere with the cook, if it was right to do so. She is your hired servant, and owes you obedience. If you banished every drop of wine, liquor, beer of any kind, from your family, you would at least know that no more drunkards would be made there."

"Every drop?" gasped Aunt Debby. "Why, the butler, the cook, and Mrs. Jillet would surely leave me."

"Others could take their places; and it is better to lose servants than to lose souls," said Miss Gale, sinking into her own corner of the carriage, much discouraged, adding: "It would be a great mercy to dear P., and you would feel that you had done your part to keep him from intemperate habits. One cannot be too careful in training a child."

"To be sure not. I shall talk to P. when I hear him say his prayers. But banish everything of the kind, and be unlike everybody! set oneself up against society! How very singular!"

It was one of Aunt Debby's misfortunes that she was unequal to every emergency of her life.

One of the first advantages of Mrs. Green's accident was that Teddy was comfortably dressed, and sent to school daily, being permitted to exercise his talent for boot-blacking during the intervals of study.

The worshipful Master Dean had a new enjoyment springing in the arid desert of his pleasure-scorched life, when he conducted Teddy to a tailor's establishment, and, after a few hints from Miss Gale, bought a suit of clothes for him; then went to the bookstore for the school-books; and finally escorted him to the school-room, and consigned him to his teacher. It was so delightful to have a *protegé* as old and as large as himself, and moreover a proficient in boot-blacking!

Our P. had got to be twelve years old, and had outgrown his governess. The guardians said he must be sent to school with other boys. He was given a gold watch and chain; he bought desk, portfolio, writing-case, books, et ceteras unnumbered; he was enrolled among the pupils of Professor Easy, and received with the adulation and respect due to a million.

Until the day when it was decided that he should go to school, poor P. was ready to die of *ennui;* life seemed to him unutterably *long*. When he read in his Bible on Sunday to Aunt Debby, that "the years of men's life are threescore years and ten," he wondered in his soul what men found to do in all that time. He coincided with David's view, that their strength was labor and sorrow. With the rapidity of Young America he had rushed through Solomon's experience, and found all vanity and vexation of spirit. The horse had become an old story; he was weary of swimmimg; the fish would not bite; and

Teddy was so sturdily matter-of-fact, that it was no fun to patronize him. Story-books had lost their entertainment; he had outgrown tops, marbles, and fancy toys; his knife cut his fingers, and his soul loathed sweetmeats; he had eaten the good things of this life *ad nauseam;* finally, he wished he was dead; he had worn out the delights of organ-grinder and monkey, and would have been glad if he had never been born—though that seems a curious possibility.

Now came the glory of going to school, and P.'s spirits revived. Alas! if he had only entered without the prestige of his fortune; if he had been put on the footing of common boys, and had to work his own way up in plays and studies! But, no; his wealth was around about him like the nimbus of the gods. He went and came with royal disregard of rules. He was a king above all law.

When P. went on the playground he was allowed to choose the game, and, whether he played well or ill, he was applauded—this, not because boys are so alive to the claims of money, but they are awake to money's worth; and P. made every day a treat of nuts, confections, nicknacks, and gingerbeer.

In the school-room, he, singularly enough, got to the head of the class when he recited well, and did not come down when he failed. The master never took up the accusative against him when he had forgotten the dative; he got perfects whether or no. The tutor corrected his exercises, and remarked that they were admirably well done; and no worry was made about his learning interest, partial payments, and compound numbers, which indeed were likely to be of little use as regarded his own fortune—that being in the hands of administrators.

CHAPTER SIXTH.

How the Young Ladies helped Matters.

"She showed a face
With dangers rife."

"She spoke, and lo! her loveliness
Methought she damaged with her tongue;
And every sentence made it less,
So false they rung."

CHAPTER SIXTH.

How the Young Ladies Helped Matters.

MASTER DEAN wandered out of the regions of childhood satiated with petting. Childhood was no fairyland to him; reality had left no room for imagination. One of the greatest delights of early days is to invent. It is not so much luxury to own a real elephant, as to make an elephant of a chair, or a big brother, draped in a table-cloth. One does not so much care to be bought a balloon, as to strive for days to make a balloon of paste and paper. The joy is not to go to the theatre, and come home sick and sleepy, but to dramatize *Mother Hubbard* or *Dame Crumb*, and play it out in spite of difficulties, with the barn, or the back bedroom, to serve for the grand building with flowers and footlights. The trouble with our boy-millionaire was, that he never was allowed to long for anything; never to toil to obtain; never to wait. The Genius of the Lamp brought him everything on the instant, and the real Aladdin was far less happy than the imaginary one.

When from childhood our P. passed to youth, new gratifications awaited him, just as likely to be worn out as the toys that had gone before. Aunt Debby had loved and petted her boy—she idolized the young man. P. had a natural gallantry and courtesy, which was agreeable to others, and pleasing to himself in its exercise; and Aunt Debby was truly enchanted with his winning ways.

P. did not, like Solomon, give himself "to seek and to search out by wisdom concerning all things that are done under heaven." Learning in "Professor Easy's Genteel Establishment for Young Men" had been made so very smooth and effortless, that there had been no pleasure in acquisition. P. rejected with scorn the idea of going to college, but gave himself quite devotedly to novel reading. P.'s grandfather Dean had built a room for a library, but he did not know what to put into it. P. solved the difficulty readily, and found books to fill the vacant shelves. We are sorry that his books were, many of them, of a questionable character.

P. tried some of Solomon's plans for killing time. He had a conservatory and an aviary; instead of the gardens and orchards, he got him fast horses and bijou turnouts, and had a morsel of a gingerbread house just out of town, which was divided into billiard-room, supper-room, and smoking-room, and where he took friends as fast as himself, for a forlorn sort of excitement, which they loathed for its unsatisfactoriness, but did not dare to say so, their pleasure being merely ashes and bitterness, although they hid the fact in their hearts.

P. had musical instruments, also like Solomon. He ruined a good piano, and made the fortune of an Italian teacher, failing to learn to play even the simplest exercises. He also had flutes and violins, wherewith he made night hideous. As for "the men singers and women singers," we must not suppose our young friend to have been behindhand. He went to the theatre and opera with great diligence; had his favorite Stars, of whom he spoke familiarly; invited them to suppers and to drives; amazed his Aunt Debby by bowing and speaking to the strangest acquaintances.

For sheer lack of amusement, our young friend might have taken to backing prize-fighters, going to races, appreciating dog-fights and cock-fights, and reading *The New York Clipper*, had not the ladies taken him in charge when he reached the age of eighteen.

P. was rich, amiable, polished in manners, handsome in person, and unexceptionable in dress. He was patronized by fashionable young married ladies, and by elderly belles. He was too young to think of marrying, and the girls from whom he could have selected a wife were yet in the nursery. He should have been in college getting ballast for that light mind of his, now setting sail on seas of folly. Instead of being at college, learning the "ics" and the "ologies," Master P. went abroad cultivating the art of flirtation. Here was the hour when a good woman, sister or friend, might have been P.'s salvation; instead, women who "meant no harm," and did no good, were likely to be his ruin. Some fair counsellor might have given this lad's life a grand aim; might have shown him the responsibilities of his position; urged him to a noble ambition; bound him to the practice of sobriety—but no such counsellor appeared. Aunt Debby, being as weak as she was well-meaning, as soon as manhood dawned in her nephew, believed him capable of guiding himself, and far more judicious than she was; so, flattered his abundant vanity, by applauding all that he did, and appealing to his judgment on every occasion. The friends of the Deans were rich and fashionable, a shining circle of dress and display; but the family of the rich liquor-dealer had not penetrated those circles where brain, and good-breeding, and moral greatness, stand supreme. There were noble women in the city, any one of whom, as guide and friend, could have led P. on to the "wisdom which excelleth folly as light excelleth darkness;" but, ah me! they did not know our boy.

For these other sirens, what shall I say of them? They were of the ninety-and-nine half-educated butterflies of society, who deem that woman's only mission is to claim admiration by a fair face or a pleasing manner. Degrading thus themselves and their own mission, it was not to be expected that they could elevate young Dean by anything they might say or do. These luckless triflers, whose first thought was dress, and whose chief desire was to obtain a gaze of adulation, learned only in the art of setting themselves off to good advantage, might have served very well as lay figures for milliner or mantua-maker, but could not have risen even to the place of "moral wax-works."

Our boy! our poor boy! He had had no mother's love and true example; he had had no sister faithful in reproof, and tender with comfort. All he knew of womanhood was here; an image more or less fair; the head, a triumph of the barber over impossibilities; the dress, a marvel from the *modiste;* laugh trained to ripple out at every nothing; apt in the dance, her only learning; and when she spoke—

"The rallying voice, the light demand,
Half flippant, half unsatisfied:
The vanity sincere and bland;
The answers wide."

The young man who learns to speak lightly on womanhood is in sore danger, but so P. learned, and we cannot wonder at it. But while teaching P. nothing that was good, these young women were sowing seeds of evil. They spoke of fashionable novels of the day; and P. discerned that their hero was not the man of honest worth, but the reckless, dashing blade. They laughed at lavish expenditure; applauded the furious driving that periled life and limb; and thought it a merry joke when the rich man trampled on the laws they claimed should only have been made for the poor. But more than this, these girls' white hands filled the wine-cup and passed the decanter; and their eyes shining with excitement of dance and music, challenged even such a lad as P., whom they made a pet and a *protegé*, to drink again and again as toasts went round.

"O, surely, Mr. Dean, you'll drink with *me!*"

"What! refuse to drink *my* health? What a shame!"

"No, sir; I'll not let you go in that way. That is *my* toast, and you are to drink it, like a friend."

Up in the crystal swelled the pink curaçoa, shedding its color back on the soft, ringed hand that held the glass. Presented thus, the maraschino had an appeal more potent than its taste or its sparkle. P. knew not that each of these bright priestesses at the shrine of Pleasure was evoking a tremendous devil that slept in his soul. He could not see that these taper fingers, jewel-set, were digging wide his early grave; and he did not hear in the tinkle of glasses, as the healths went round, the rattle of stone and thud of sod upon an unblessed coffin. Here, in this glittering sea of fashionable dissipation, P. was lured by the song of the sirens of the enchanted and fatal isle, and he was no brave Ulysses, to stop his ears and go safely by.

The first time that ever P. got drunk—stupid, dead, inert from liquor—was at a birthday ball of one of these belles, where all seemed bent on the poor lad's destruction.

He had not ordered his own carriage to come for him, and going home in one with others overtaken by the strength of wine, they managed to get him laid on his own doorway, but were all, coachman and companions, too drunk to remember to ring the bell. P. might have shocked the genteel neighborhood by lying there until morning—for though genteel people will make their friends and fellow-citizens drunk, they do not wish them to display their drunkenness in public—he might even have frozen, like Nurse Green's baby; but Teddy Green, going home late from a printing-office where he worked, saw him, and was moved, not alone by humanity, but by certain affection for one who, since childhood, had shown him many favors. Teddy succeeded in rousing Mrs. Jillet and the butler, and by their aid got the youthful master of the house to bed.

Next morning P., on awakening, felt some shame and self-reproach, a little of dread as to the habit he might be forming. There was a fine chance for some one to make an impression, but in this world need and opportunity are often far asunder. There was no one to speak to P. but Mrs. Jillet. *She* came in early, bringing a glass of brandy and water.

"And how are you this morning, sir? Here's something to set you up nicely. La, now, don't look like *that.* Why, it is nothing but what befalls every gentleman as is a gentleman. Bless me! but you'll get used to it; no use in being so squeamish about trifles. Oh, dear me! you're not so old yet as you will be, and youth is the time for enjoyment, as I was telling Mrs. Bently. There now, that's gone, shall I bring you a drop more, or anything else at all? No? Best go to sleep again, sir, and you'll be fresh as a lark by noon."

P.'s next social disaster arose from the custom of New Year's calls. This is a fashion we inherited from our Dutch ancestors in the good city of Manhattan, who went about from house to house to wish the inmates a good year, and were received by the notable housewives with a treat of "*oley koeks*" and other goodies. It was a kindly custom; but, unless there is soon a new order of exercises connected with it, it will be "more honored in the breach than in the observance."

"Of course, my dear boy," remarked Aunt Debby, "you will be very careful what you take to-day. I was pained to see that many of the gentlemen who came to call on me last New Year's were nearly intoxicated."

"To be sure," said P., indifferently. "Every one knows it is dangerous mixing liquors; and some folks have the vilest trash, which they believe to be good port and brandy, because they have paid a big price for it. I believe there is not a drop of real port wine in the country, except what is in my cellar. Then you know, aunt, 'many littles make a mickle;' and when one takes a glass or half a glass, or even a taste, at each of a hundred calling-places, he can't help being overloaded."

'Dear, dear! Well, P., my son, you must refuse at some of the places."

"That is easier said than done. There would be a cry, 'O, you must try *my* wine.' 'Refuse some one else, you won't find as good champagne anywhere.' 'Ah, now you are slighting *me*, and that is too bad.' O, you see, aunt, one cannot refuse any of the dear creatures, and so one goes home drunk."

"Why, it is a great pity," said Aunt Debby, sincerely. "I wish some way might be found to do differently."

"The way is clear enough," replied P. "If only the ladies wouldn't offer us drink, we would not be drunk. What do they have the stuff brought on for?"

"Every one would make remarks on our penuriousness, and lack of hospitality, if we offered no wine," said Miss Dean, with the utmost innocence.

"O, yes; and for fear we fellows would sneer—and we would not, for the half of us would be glad from the bottom of our souls if we were not given a drop—you women run the risk of sending us to sleep in the station-house."

"The station-house! Oh, my dear boy, don't suggest such a thing; you really frighten me!"

When P., in magnificent array, came down the staircase to set out on his round of calls, he had a view of his aunt's refection splendidly set forth in the second drawing-room. Bottles and decanters and glasses glittered on a side-table. Aunt Debby was about to do her share in making drunkards. She sat in the reception-room, a lovely, elderly gentlewoman; one never saw softer hands, nor a kindlier smile; there was not a fault to be found with her appearance from top to toe. You might say the same of her intention; it was perfectly good; not a flaw in it; she never meant the least harm; she lived in friendship with all men and women—which is saying a good deal for her—and yet from her house flowed one of those rills of evil influence which are poisoning the land.

Aunt Debby went to the window to watch her boy set off. He had a radiant little shell of a sleigh, with wolf-skin robes; his pair of prancing black horses seemed to appreciate the beauty of the silver-mounted harness, and the clear ringing of their many bells. The young owner had mounted for the first time a stiff, high silk hat; his fur coat had been especially imported for him, and was a Christmas gift from Auut Debby. Beside him sat a grinning black boy, in brillant livery, who rolled his eyes, and showed his teeth, in the joy of expectation. A stout, respectably-dressed fellow, with a quick step and honest face, came by, and cheerily wished "A happy New Year." It was Teddy Green, who had helped print P.'s morning paper this year past. He was going home now, with a cap and a shawl for a present to his grandmother, who had grown so old that she could only sit and doze in her big chair, yet not too old to love Teddy. The lad had come out of his way in hopes of getting a look at P., whom he sincerely loved. Taking the look, with fond pride in his friend's grandeur, he felt a fear that the return might be less glorious than the going forth.

All day long the round of conventional good wishes, the well-worn compliments, the trite responses, the carefully-conned joke and repartee. P. thought it all vastly entertaining, for this was but his second venture in New Year's calls, and last year he had made his essay in company with one of his guardians. Long before day was done, P. wished cookery an undiscovered art; he was ready to anathematize each new invention of the kitchen; and loathed what he felt bound to praise. As to wine and other drinkables of dangerous variety and quality, the fumes were mounting to his head. The very elegant mother who pressed upon him a taste of her sherry, felt compelled to notice to herself that the young man was getting tipsy. Anna Medora, who sweetly handed him a julep, wondered if P. would not be a very fast young man, and what his aunt would say if he went home staggering; and Miss Mary Amanda, with ten years' experience of belledom, told him her papa was quite proud of his Madeira, would he try some? and considered the ways of young men very devious, and thought it a pity that they would be dissipated.

Nightfall before the last call was finished; and with an unsteady step P. went down from the last marble portico, wondering what had happened to his hat—he having taken the wrong headgear from a servant as tipsy as himself—able to discover that the world goes round, if Galileo had not been before him.

P. was warm enough, but the stinging winter air put the black horses on their mettle; they pranced along, and P. performed absurd feats of driving. The splendidly-arrayed black boy had probably been treated by admiring maid servants; he was stupidly intoxicated, and, giving a chuckle, rolled ignominiously out into the snow. P. drove on without missing his boy, and, taking any streets where his horses happened to go, was at last inspired to interfere with their motions, and drove them furiously at a lamp-post, bringing the shell of a sleigh to untimely ruin. Away went the horses, dragging a fragment of the wreck. Our P sat on the curbstone, his fur cloak and fashionable boots in the slush of the sewer, not moralizing, but laughing loudly at the adventure.

In an hour's time, if you had sought the city over for Mr. P. Dean, millionaire, ward of two first-class guardians and the Orphans' Court, prey of three administrators, and source of emolument to six legal gentlemen, you would have found him nowhere else but in a station-house! He was not alone; he was locked up with three other makers of New Year's calls, each quite as respectable and refined as himself. A little light struggled in over the door from an outer room, and showed P. draggled and rumpled; hat and gloves gone; boots wet; fur dripping; seated on a hard bench; braced uneasily against the wall; still finding the world going round at a perilous rate, and himself in danger of being spun off into infinite space, falling and falling for ever more.

"Them's a rum set of young bloods to take up in a police court to-morrow morning," said one policeman to another. "Watches and diamond rings on 'em. Won't there be a trying to hush it up!"

"Poor lads!" said an elderly man, compassionately. "I'll venture not one of them meant a bit of harm when he set out this morning. It has all come of meeting their good wishes with a glass of poison. These mothers and sisters are deliberately killing their neighbors' sons and brothers. It would save us a heap of trouble on New Year's Day if there was a city ordinance forbidding offering wine and such liquors for refreshments."

CHAPTER SEVENTH.

Help from the Heavy Fathers.

"Hundreds of men were turned to beasts,
Like the guests at Circe's horrible feasts,
By the magic of ale and cider:
And each country lass, and country lad,
Began to caper and dance like mad;
And even some old ones appeared to have had
A bite from the Naples spider."

CHAPTER SEVENTH.

Material Aid of Heavy Fathers.

DURING the eighteen years of his orphanage, P. had doubtless received many favors and courtesies from his guardians and administrators, earnest of good deeds yet to be done in his behalf. Friendship had first been shown by handsful of bon-bons to the boy in petticoats; it came next in the guise of miniature uniforms, guns and swords, fireworks, magic lanterns, and engines that wound up with keys and springs, presented to the round-faced lad; the horse and the phaeton followed, and when at sixteen, P. with much shame-facedness and secret pride put on his first long-tailed coat, a splendid glossy plum-colored broadcloth; he was duly invited to Saratoga and Cape May, by administrator No. 1, J. Pincham, Sr. Saratoga had not then been blessed with a Member of Congress to open a gambling-saloon for the improvement of the youth who flocked thither to learn good manners, morals, and statesmanship; but father

Pincham found means to make P.'s hours pass pleasantly and unprofitably.

The dancing-master had faithfully performed his part, and the "fantastic toe" of young P. was the most fantastic of its sort. The young man was able to kill the time between ten and two, when old-fashioned people were sound asleep, with unnumbered round dances, with Sybil or Seraphina. When these dear creatures had left the glare of the gaslight, and soared to higher regions, in the third or fourth stories, P. had the wine-room to revisit, and like a lad of spirit must take a cigar in the smoking-room; it was late when he found time to sleep, and nearly noon when he came down stairs to try the waters of his favorite spring, and get his breakfast.

Well removed from the rest of the public rooms, was a snug apartment whither J. Pincham, Sr., often beguiled the ward of the Orphans' Court, and benevolently initiated him into the science of card-playing. P. had heretofore learned one card from another, and with more or less judgment handed them over, in parlor games of euchre and whist; but now he learned a depth of which he had not dreamed, he was instructed to gamble as became a gentleman, and father Pincham blandly won his money, "just to show him how the thing was done;" he kept it with the same wise intention. The skilful management of the "pasteboards" was invariably accompanied by sips of brandy and water; the brandy became more, the water less, and the *sips* enlarged to drinks as time went on.

Later in P.'s day, driving was in order; and fancy driving, dashing horses, stylish turnouts, racing and betting, and quarrelling over different beasts, and the choice vocabulary of the stables, formed a part of the education for which this young man was deeply indebted to the administrator.

In the early evening the consequential, bloated, and profoundly self-satisfied Pincham, Sr., and our boy, fresh and slender, with already a weary, wondering look at the tiresome shams he had found in life, seated in close conversation, might have moved the soul of a philanthropist. The elder man was fat-faced, small-eyed and leering; he had a huge ring on his little finger, and a ponderous seal on his watch chain; he settled his big head comfortably in his collar, and though he said but little, each speech seemed somehow a long step toward the devil, whom this man was ever ready to meet half way. P. had the innocent frankness of early life; however sick he might be of the present, he was dowered with the future, the heritage of all youth. Of this he spoke;

he would do thus and so, buy, sell, journey, enjoy, in those halcyon days when he had come of age and received his own.

"All this will take a vast deal of money,' said his mature companion.

"But I have a great deal; a million is a deal of money," said P., with calm assurance.

"That is true, but you do not reckon the expenses of your establishment, and education all these years."

"Those are out of the income," said P., acutely. "The expenses cannot possibly now outrun the income."

"Expenses are very heavy," said Pincham, puffing out clouds of smoke.

"And the income is very great," insisted P.

"O yes, certainly," replied the administrator. "You are doubtless a rich man, still you know, legal fees and so forth eat great holes, and moreover estates rarely ever foot up to the first estimate."

If P. had been reasonably trained, these remarks would have set him thinking. But P. did not like to take the trouble to think; he left that to Professor Easy, and others who were paid for it; moreover his cigar made him stupid, cards and brandy had set his brain in a whirl, and there was a ball in prospect.

These days at Saratoga were 'ess innocent, and

truly less happy, than the quiet years when Aunt Debby with her pale, loving face had bent over his bed to hear his evening prayer; had kissed him, and bade him be a good boy; and on Sunday had taken him duly to church and had him read her a chapter from the Bible when they got home. If only Aunt Debby had known how to be consistent, or if she had worked as well as wished!

In the city the Orphan was neglected neither by his own nor his father's friends. He began to be invited to dinner parties, and remained—greatly bored—to drink wine on occasions when he would have been better pleased with the society of the ladies; the young man having arrived at the sentimental stage of his existence.

After these dinners P. sometimes went home simply tired, and wondering what good there was in living; but once in a while, being young and as yet unused to these occasions, he left his host and his wits at the same time, and wandered about maudlin, and in a half frenzy, getting home rather by good luck than good management.

Peregrinating the streets in this unsteady fashion, and trolling forth a stave of a popular song, P. attracted the notice of Teddy Green, our young gentleman having wandered away from the aristocratic locality of his own abode, and intruded into the quarter of respectable poverty, where, if people are out late, it is because they are at their work. P. was so excited in mind, and so unsteady on his legs, that Teddy thought the only sensible course was to take him to his own humble abode, and let him seek the lofty Dean mansion when he got better. These foster brothers accordingly climbed a high staircase, and Teddy helping P. to the bed, considerately laid himself upon the floor, with his coat wrapped up for a pillow. P.'s last remark at night was that Teddy was "a gay old boy, and here's your health, sir!"

When he woke in the morning he missed the gorgeous canopy, the down-filled quilt, the rosewood and marble, the dainty appliances of the toilette, which had ever greeted his opening eyes.

Instead, he saw the four-post cherry-wood bedstead, the patchwork coverlet, the windows with newspapers for curtains, a windsor chair, a box covered with chintz, doing duty as a dressing-table, a square stand with a brown bowl and pitcher, a crash towel and a square of bar soap, which all looked so amazingly primitive and absurd, that P. sat up in bed and shouted with laughter, and so sitting up came in view of Mr. Teddy laid on the floor, with no ceremony of undressing but pulling off his boots and unbuttoning his vest, his head resting on a rolled-up coat, and making a spread eagle of himself, with arms extended and fists clenched; P. laughed louder and louder.

Teddy woke up and smiled, but grimly.

"Well, Teddy, my lad, here's a jolly go? How came I here? am I visiting you, or are we both visiting some one else? or has Uncle Sam taken us both up in some moment of unconsciousness, and landed us in one of his favorite institutions?"

"If you please, Mr. Dean, such moments of unconsciousness do not come to me," said Teddy. "This is my room; and, though it suits me very properly, I'm sorry it is not better for you."

"And how, in the name of wonder, did I get here?"

"I found you coming along the street, sir, not over well able to take care of yourself, and I made you as easy as I could."

"Ah, I remember something about it. So we were *both* out late, it seems, Ted, my boy?"

"I was out for business, sir, getting ready your paper; and you were out for what they call *pleasure*, but of a poor sort; for, if only that is well that ends well, this must be ill enough."

"Yes, yes, to be sure. I went to dinner with that

confounded Snell, one of my administrators, Teddy. Sometimes I wish there had been nothing to administer upon. Between the fathers and the daughters, and the rest of them, I'm like to go to the dogs, Teddy, as you poor rascals are too busy to go. And you stick to the paper yet? Printer's devil, or what are you now?"

"I'm a compositor," said Teddy, gruffly.

"Keep bad hours, don't you, Teddy? We rich villains can lie abed until noon; but I did not know you could try it."

"Late work and late sleep, sir," replied Teddy. "If you'd honor us by stopping to breakfast, we can give you a good one. Mother's got over that trouble she fell into at your house, and we do right well once more."

"That's good news," said P., cordially, dropping back on his pillow. "Yes; I'll stay. It will be something new; and a change is what I'm dying for. How many are there of you, Teddy?"

"There's grandmother; she's old as old can be, but we make her quite happy. And there's father; he's just more than contented. Mother; she's good as gold, *now*. There's my big brother, clerk at the grocer's; he's talking of getting married. And there's a little sister, four years old; we're making up to her for the trouble that happened the other little one. Then here I am; I mean not to stop until I'm an editor."

Teddy had got up, pulled off part of his clothes, and now soused his head and neck thoroughly in a basin of water; he turned, his face and hair dripping, as he reached for the towel. "We are a temperance family now, sir, and I recommend it to you. If you had cold-water principles, you would not be dying for a change, and find living such a bore as you do. If you had a clear brain, that no liquors heated up, you'd take to doing something; and work brings rest and a glad heart—that it does. Do you know, I think every man owes the world a man's work; and the richer and wiser we are, the more's our duty to do something. I remember you from when we were both small fellows, and I blacked your boots. You have done me many a good turn; and if I only could make a cold-water man of you, Mr. Dean, I'd feel as if I'd paid all I owed."

"Don't talk of *owing;* there was nothing but my own pleasure in my mind, Teddy. But it is quite enough to make one shiver, to see you washing yourself this November morning between two open windows. Why, Teddy, it makes me laugh to hear you talk of temperance. No one but you ever mentioned the matter to me: and consider the amount of teachers, and guardians, and legal advisers and doctors I've had about me."

"'Too many cooks spoil the broth,'" growled Teddy, as he brought fresh water and towels, and put the windows down, that the dainty P. might dress himself, while Teddy helped his mother get breakfast.

The father had been off to work this some time, and the breakfast was only for the two—a gala affair; ham and eggs, apple-sauce, fried potatoes, and corn-bread. Mrs. Green did her best; and Teddy, with an honest appetite ever at command, thought it wonderful. Even P. ate heartily, and questioned within himself why they could not get up as good a breakfast at home; he meant to speak on the subject to the obsequious Mrs. Jillet. Whether it was the hard bed, the freezing water, and the frosty morning air, to which Teddy had treated him, or the newness of the cookery, P. could not have told, but something made him hungry; and, as he ate, he cast curious glances at his foster-mother.

Mrs. Green could never regain the comely proportions, and the traditional milkmaid innocence, which she had taken to the Dean mansion; but for these seven or eight years she had been a reformed woman, and her household rejoiced in her restoration. Miss

Gale had been the means through which this blessing had come to the family, and P. had heretofore heard of it from Teddy, and from the ex-governess herself. As he sat at the table that morning, he felt it was a work worthy of her; for he honored Miss Gale above all the women he had ever seen. The beauty of her life was its consistency; she so thoroughly practised what she preached. The first point was to ascertain duty; the next was to do it.

Breakfast over, and Teddy setting off to his work, P. prepared to return home.

"Won't Miss Dean be frightened at your absence?" asked Teddy.

P. laughed at the idea of alarm on his account.

"She will probably not know it. If she does—why, she is used to it."

"Not from this same cause, I hope?" said Teddy, seriously.

"O, no, not often; to be sure not. I'm a pretty straight fellow, after all. Not so prim as you are, but well in a way. I stay out sometimes from one cause, sometimes from another. No one ever asks me why; the dear old soul would be afraid of offending. I often wish, Ted, that there had been somebody to call me to an account in all this world. It might have been better."

"That is so," said Teddy, with solemnity. "It might serve to make you better prepared for a grand account we must all render some day; higher up, you know."

P. walked on, with his head down, pondering. At last he spoke: "I think there's a good deal of excuse for me. You have no idea, Teddy, how hard it is on a fellow to be brought up as I have been. Every one seems to have tried to make me selfish and shiftless. Never anything to do; and everything I wanted handed over at once. I often wish I'd had a million cents, instead of a million dollars."

"There's no use wishing to throw away your privileges, Mr. Dean. The Lord gave you a fortune to be used like a man and a Christian; and if its possession brings you many temptations, you should only try harder to overcome them. The great danger with you, sir, is strong drink. If you'd only let that alone."

"If I *only* would! O, Teddy, how little you know! I'm waylaid and besieged by it on every hand. From the day I was born until now I have been beset by it. Cooks and doctors, friends and relations, old and young, men and women, they tempt me—tempt me all the time. And, Teddy, if I do yield, and am sometimes the worse for drinking, I really think those who make it, and sell it, and offer it, are more to blame than I am."

"It is no use questioning who is the most blamable, sir. The first thing is to keep your own account clear, and to beware of what is wrong. If you only had some object in life——"

"Haven't any, Teddy. Never could find one; and living is very tedious, after all. Sometimes I wish I could jump out of it."

"Like your father before you," said Teddy to himself, as he nodded good morning, and turned down toward the office where he worked, leaving the poor young millionaire to saunter toward the home of whose luxury he was so weary.

Administrators Pincham and Snell, doing their part against Master Dean, Administrator Binkle, an old bachelor of more means than reputation, took a share in the proceedings. Mr. Binkle was of good family—not that the Binkles had ever been shining lights, mentally or morally, but they had made money in land speculations for several generations. Binkle having been brought up to fashionable proprieties, had in his mature years darted off into Bohemianism. His house was a favorite rendezvous for fourth-rate wits and painters; for the composers of love-songs and contributors to flash papers. Actors and singers and ballet-dancers of a low degree found in Binkle a patron; and into their choice society Binkle brought his youthful friend, Aunt Debby's boy and darling.

Once again life opened something new to the victim of good fortune. He had hitherto sat in a private box, and watched the play played out; he now could get behind the scenes, into the green-room, at rehearsal, and see the making-up, the miffs and mistakes, the tinsel and folly; and he wondered to find how sick he grew of it all. How he pitied those who must drearily make bread and butter by these miseries day after day!

"Don't you wish," said P. to an actor who had been assassinated a score of days in succession, "don't you wish that it had been real, and no farce, and you were done with the bother of existence?"

The man meditated a little. "Well, no. The fact is *I* have something to live for—failure to dread—success to desire—a support to obtain. I have the advantage of you there, Mr. Dean. You are the most completely bored person I ever met. Life has been made too easy to you. We complain about the thorns on the roses; yet, after all, I sometimes wonder if the thorns are not an attraction."

P. had thought of dropping out of his own circle

and joining a theatrical company; but then, as he could not have lost the possibility of returning to his fortune, he would still have had no spur to exertion—and it would have been so tiresome to learn his part!

Perhaps if we were to point out one place more than another, where the chains of intemperance were riveted on our P., we would fix on the house of Binkle, for here more fiery and abundant potations were indulged in. Here they drank, not for fashion's sake, fashionable drinks, to criticise, to praise, or to condemn; but they drank from a feverish thirst—a love of the liquor itself. P. wondered that they found anything so desirable in these drinks, but he was lured on to try for himself.

"Young man," said Dr. Roxwell, "you are living at a 2-40 rate. You have been living fast ever since you were born. You are now some ten years my senior—and the family Bible shows me sixty my last birthday."

CHAPTER EIGHTH.

The Law does its Part.

"Old Mother Hubbard went to her cupboard,
To get her old dog a bone.
When she got there, the cupboard was bare,
And so the poor dog got none."

CHAPTER EIGHTH.

The Law does its Part.

WE are told that Mother Hubbard's dog was "her only care;" the result, so far as we have been able to gather from credible historians, was his sudden and mysterious demise. P. was the care of three administrators, two guardians, six gentlemen learned in law, Dr. Roxwell, Aunt Debby, and the Orphans' Court. Under the supervision of these thirteen individuals, *and* the said Court, our infant attained his majority, and stood forth a man and a fellow-citizen.

In the few months before this great event, Aunt Debby was in a flutter of expectations; she indeed hoped so much, anticipated so much, made so many fine preparations for presents and festival to celebrate the birth of the Heir of a Million, that she fell ill, and was forced to call in Dr. Roxwell.

"Ah! my dear doctor," said the amiable Aunt Debby, "you do not know how I have hoped for the day that is now drawing near. I expect my boy to do a great deal of good with his money. Once he is master of himself, my dear P. will show what is in him. He is the most charitable creature that ever was known. Did you hear of all he did for that Green family? Saved them in fact, the darling!"

Now we will say for young Dean, that he had never thought of giving his aunt this high idea of his good deeds, when he had mentioned the Green household in her presence. Aunt Debby's love, as is love's wont, had outrun facts.

"And what particular good deed do you plan for your nephew, now that he has got done with the Green family?" asked Dr. Roxwell, dryly.

"I have had my mind very much on an asylum for genteel people of decayed fortunes. We could call it the DEAN INSTITUTE, and it would ever remain a memorial to the family. I would not wish a shabby, close, narrow sort of place, to be for ever reminding people how poor they are; but a handsome house, in a pleasant garden; with well-furnished rooms; a library; and say a couple of coaches for people to get out sometimes. When people grow to my age, dear doctor, they get tired of fashion and society, and find it far more congenial to busy themselves in doing good. I know I do; and my sympathies are very much enlisted for nice people who have seen better days."

"Well, I confess that my charities would take the direction of such poor forsaken little wretches as have seen no good days at all, and, from no fault of their own, have been starving on husks ever since they formed a distinct part of creation. But, Miss Dean, I wish to bring before you a subject which has greatly occupied my mind lately. Do you know, that of estates that go into the hands of administrators and executors, a large proportion never reach the heirs? They melt away, filtering into somebody's pocket, of course, but diverted from the original intention."

"I don't see how that can be, doctor," said Aunt Debby. "When so many people are provided to look after property, it *must* be well taken care of."

"There is no such necessity in fact," replied the doctor. "A piece of porcelain is much more likely to be broken in being handed about among a company than when held by one person. When a great fortune, or a little fortune, is looking for care-takers, and those who have the handling of it are bound to feather their nests, then *I* say, the fewer the better."

"There's the Orphans' Court to look after everybody."

"And Courts bring legal expenses. Now I know very little what direction these affairs of young Dean are taking; but I do say this: Since Messrs. Pincham, Snell, and Binkle are to make money out of him; since two guardians will scrupulously look out for their own interests; since six lawyers have had fees through twenty-one years of service; you need hardly expect your nephew to have means to found, endow, and sustain a genteel asylum, unless, indeed, he is to take refuge in it himself."

"Why, sir," said Aunt Debby, nervously, "in my experience, people always get their own."

"Your experience, Miss Dean," said the doctor, calmly, "is only that of those women whose status in society is as if they were done up in cotton, and kept in a glass case. I question if you know anything at all of the hard facts of existence. One fact is, that executors, or those who serve for them, inherit the major part of estates, the interest of the true heirs being so sedulously looked after that it becomes nothing at all. Men toil and strive; peril their souls to get money; often pinch and hamper their children, that they may leave a larger fortune, and what is the result? Generally, just this: That some of their neighbors and relations step in to make matters straight, and they keep paring and cutting away until all is gone. It is like old Æsop's fable of the division of the cheese; the arbitrator bit first one piece and then the other, to make them even, and so kept on biting until all was gone; and the two expectants got nothing but leave to go off howling."

"Indeed, Dr. Roxwell, I have always read that—that——"

"You have read that on attaining their majority, the heirs come into possession with great *éclat.* That only happens in novels, my dear madam. Real experience is that the cupboard is bare, and the dog—albeit he looked for nothing but a bone—gets none."

"What a misfortune for minor children to lose their parents!" said Aunt Debby, plaintively.

"The case is even worse for grown-up children, very frequently," said the doctor, settling himself quite comfortably in his easy-chair. "I have often talked it over to my cousin Nancy. The guardian and the administrator of the minor feels that he has some time in which to work for himself before accounts must be rendered; and meantime, to keep matters quiet, he takes care of the juvenile owner of the property he means to seize. The heir gets that much good out of his estate. But I have known sons and daughters who had reached a majority to be jewed out of every copper, and obliged to pay the costs of the little operation."

"Dreadful! dreadful!" groaned Miss Dean. "But where are the bonds the Court claims, and why cannot the adult children administer the estate themselves?"

"One part of your question explains the other. The children are not administrators because of the bonds required. They cannot furnish a security; and their inheritance is therefore secured by, and to, some one else. If the children administered the estate, they might deal fairly—*would*, perhaps. I have not a high opinion of human decency; but there is the chance that fraternal feeling would cause them to divide with the co-heirs; and, at all events, there is the consolation of thinking that the property would go to *one* of those for whom it was intended."

"And yet the laws that govern the care and division of property have occupied profound legal minds these many years. Can they be improved on?" ventured poor Miss Dean, much perplexed.

"I don't know indeed. 'It's a' a muddle'—very much of a muddle. I just touched on the subject to let you know that you must not have too large views concerning the money coming to your nephew, for it is likely to dwindle down to a very trifle."

"It is terrible!" said Aunt Debby, turning pale. "It quite makes me sick to think of it."

"O, I came here to cure you, not to kill you," said the doctor. "And I dare say, after all, that I know more of medicine than of law. Things may prove different from what I suggest; and moreover I think poverty would be the very best thing in the world for our P. I am afraid, after all, that he will have enough property left to ruin him."

Nor is it odd that our dear Aunt Debby had so high an opinion of the potent dollar, that the doctor's last suggestion was a balm to her vexed spirit.

Meantime, the thoughts of Aunt Debby's nephew had turned to his estate. All his life he had been so well taught the power of money, in gratifying his whims, smoothing his way, and buying him ease and praise, that he was not now likely to despise it. If his planning about what he would do with it was a little different from Aunt Debby's, we must consider his youth, and the indulgence he had received.

As the last six months of his minority rolled away, our young man found something to do, instructing administrators, guardians, and lawyers that he meant to have his business punctually settled, accounts rendered, and claims met, on the grand day when he should be one-and-twenty. If this should not be done, how in the world did this rash young fellow mean to mend matters, but by feeing another lawyer on his own behalf, and carrying the business again into Court!

Poor fellow! he was credulous and ardent; but then—he was young, and deliciously ignorant of law!

Of course during two decades these administrators and guardians had known that a day would dawn which would prove a day of account, either in this world or the next; but both seemed equally remote, and they had failed to prepare for the occasion. To begin with the administrators, they were rascals of a diverse fashion. For instance:—

Binkle's rascality was that of indifference. He had suffered himself to be made one of the administrators of the Dean Million, because it was so much trouble to refuse, and he had been assured that he should not be bored with business. Binkle had his actors, poets, new plays, and sham tragedies to attend to. He said to P.: "My dear fellow, I really don't know a word about this business. Go to Pincham; he does the work. I don't even look on. A settlement? O, certainly; they're easy enough to get at, ain't they? Pincham will tell you everything. I haven't had the least bother with your estate these twenty years. I left it all to him, and you'll find it by far the easiest way."

"The easiest way to get rid of other folks' con cerns, but *not* the easiest way to look out for your own," said P., sharply.

"O, well, maybe so; every one to his taste. I know no French but one verb, P., and I spend my whole existence conjugating that—*s'amuser.*"

Thus much for the erudite Binkle; and our young man addressed himself to Snell. Mr. T. Snell was one of the rascals of quiet complicity. He had no particular designs on P.'s fortune further than marrying to it one of the Misses Snell, if it should prove large enough, when paid over, to be worth the matrimonial scheming. The paternal Snell had had the orphan to Niagara, to Montreal, to Lake Champlain, and the White Mountains, in company with all the Snell family, and the expenses of the Snell family had been covered by those charged to the heir. Snell had had a pair of carriage horses, or so, through buying for the youthful orphan; and his wine, and his coachman's wages, had been met by the tremendous charges supposed to be made in the establishment of the millionaire. Snell was a little man, and his meannesses were little. He could not get up a courage to cheat like Pincham; he knew what Pincham was after, and he let him go on, provided he might get his own small stealings unmolested.

J. Pincham, Sr., had worked hard for his position as administrator, from the day when that ill-fated young Dean, P.'s father, had put a bullet into his frenzied brain. Pincham was not your man to help himself to wine, or wages, or pleasure-trips; he took his plunder by whole handfuls, by round thousands.

When P. said to Snell that he would soon be of age, would manage matters for himself, and expected to be promptly put in charge of his own property, Snell said, "Yes, yes, yes; Pincham mentioned it to me lately. Estates are a deal of trouble. Yours has been a great charge to us. We have been careful to keep your accounts, and have set down every little item—every item; and your expenses are *enormous.* Pincham is the man to do business, P., and he will make everything plain. *I* have done very little—perfect confidence in him—no time—no tact as he has. Yes, yes, yes, go to Pincham. Come dine to-morrow."

To Pincham went P. with his remarks "that they were aware, &c., and he expected, &c., and twenty-one years was a very long time."

"Well," responded this prince of rascals, "it takes a long time to straighten matters up, to make transfers, to examine accounts, to pay debts. You remember I suggested to you some four or five years ago that your expenses were absolutely prodigious, and that estates met with losses—in short, that fortunes never met expectations. Our services have been many, and gratuitous. I have done, and will do, my best for—all concerned. I hope your aunt has not been *too* extravagant." (Poor Aunt Debby!) "As a rough sketch, you have lived up the income every year. We'll say there has been a hundred thousand or so paid out to the lawyers; that another hundred thousand or so fell short in the original summing up of the estate; that a few more hundreds of thousands were lost by the big fire, when Snell had failed to reinsure, and by the wreck of the "*Polyanthus*," loaded with rum, and returning to New York from the West Indies, in the year of your father's unfortunate decease—all these items count up; but I'll do my best for all concerned, and try and save you something."

P.'s eyes were opened to a treachery, and he rushed off madly and found a lawyer to watch Mr. Pincham and pick flaws in his reports, show up his frauds, and force him to refund.

Unhappy P.! His twenty-first birthday was no more propitious than the day when he opened his eyes "to this world troublesome." He was driven and harassed by a thousand distractions; he felt that he had been foully overreached and swindled; he had not been educated in a manner to enable him to take his own part and help himself; he hated Pincham, Snell, Binkle,—everybody.

His guardians made a dinner-party, congratulated him, drank his health, wished him prosperity, and in so doing—made him drunk. They hoped their heavy cares for him were ended; and when they sent him home stupid and surly in his carriage; they said their reign over him was finished, and his own had begun.

The one guardian was an old bachelor who had done little for his ward but neglect him. He had been chosen by Aunt Debby because he was such an elegant gentleman, and made such entirely fascinating bows. Perhaps Aunt Debby had at some time silently and secretly fallen in love with this man, and worn out the unfed affection—who knows? There are a many queer things in this world.

The other guardian was also of Aunt Debby's choosing. He was an uncle of P.'s mother; he had helped himself of P.'s abundance like the rest of people. He was the father of three sons, all of whom P., quite unconsciously, had sent to college, and started in business.

When Aunt Debby found that matters had gone very wrong, and that P. had not woke up on the morning of his twenty-first birthday to find a million of dollars all in gold, piled up in his ante-room, like the Inca's ransom, as she had been rather vaguely dreaming, she laid it to the malfeasance of the guardians, and primarily to herself as having selected them. She accused herself of having beggared her idolized boy; she went to her bed inconsolable, and stayed there a month, in spite of Dr. Roxwell. We shall not say that P. did anything to console her; he was too cross from his own troubles and disappointments to care for any one.

P. went to court; he haunted law-offices; he heard opinions; he gained decisions, and when all was over he knew just this, which we shall tell you: He had exactly one hundred thousand dollars, instead of the million which had been left him. How he came to have that, he could not find out; it was explained to him a number of times, but he never understood it. It looked quite clear to him, and to everybody, that there had been a million left by the suicide Dean, twenty-one years before; where it had gone, how, to whom, was never clearly put into speech. The courts and society seemed to consider every one who had handled this property quite irreproachable; the lawyers were all honorable men; the administrators were without suspicion, especially the admirable Pincham; the guardians were incorruptible.

Nothing was said of the bonds entered into; no

one heard of any restitution imposed, or punishment deserved; there is nothing so potent as precedent, and P.'s property had gone the way that orphans' fortunes generally go.

Well, yes! the millionaire had come down to a paltry hundred thousand, he said to himself. He might still have a Miss Snell, if he wanted her.

"My dear fellow," said Dr. Roxwell, "my opinion is, that you ought to have been very glad you came of age as you did. If your minority had lasted another five years, you would have found your sole inheritance to be some ten thousand dollars' worth of debts, which would have been very heavy on you."

"And I think," sobbed Aunt Debby, "that my poor boy has been most shamefully handled, and cheated by all of them!"

"That is a common occurrence in this world; we are all like the naughty little lobsters who *will* bite their brother's legs off," said the doctor.

Miss Gale was there spending the evening; she was quietly making a gown for a little child in a hospital, and now looked up. "Do you know what *I* think? The man who made the money, your grandfather P., did not pay the Lord his tithes, and so the Lord is now doing the tithing. Do you understand, P.? Your grandfather kept back the tenths, and now you get *only* a tenth. Estates won't hold together unless they are well cemented by giving. Men gather, gather, never think of scattering to the poor; and by-and-by the grand fortune is driven about to the four winds of heaven, and the descendants have to scrabble for their little share as if they never had any claim on it. Do you suppose your father would have liked to work for Mr. Pincham, Miss Dean?"

"Why, now that I think of it, my father was always at swords' points with him," said Aunt Debby.

"By your theory, you make me suffer for the faults of my ancestors," said P. to Miss Gale.

"Children often do that," she said. "May you suffer from them no more, my poor P."

CHAPTER NINTH.

And the Devil does his.

"How widely its agencies vary,
To save—to ruin—to curse—to bless—
As even its minted coins express ;
Now stamped with the image of good Queen Bess,
And now with Bloody Mary."

CHAPTER NINTH.

And the Devil does His.

THE World, the Flesh, and the Devil, these are three things we are supposed to renounce in our baptism; these are the three enemies of the soul from the hour when it comes "trailing clouds of glory;" very soon, alas! to enter clouds of gloom. The World, the Flesh, and the Devil—these, Bunyan's Pilgrim met and conquered; the World in the City of Destruction; the Flesh in the hardships of the way, the Slough, the burdened back, the Difficult Hill, the lions lying by the path; the Devil in that Valley of Humiliation that should have been a happy place, but was not. These all the Prince of Dreamers saw—met, and worsted, in vision—we meet them, and are conquered.

Our P., with his million in expectation, had been made the slave of the world from his first breath. Aunt Debby had renounced it for him, and immediately handed him over bound hand and foot in its follies; then came the temptations of the flesh to the poor pampered boy, and he was carried captive at once of indolence, vanity, eating and drinking; and now that he was twenty-one, and his own master, the Devil came alongside, looking like an angel of light very likely, and P. surrendered.

Until the change in his fortunes, P. had seemed an easy, jolly, innocent lad, neither very good nor very evil; after getting from Pincham & Co. only one-tenth of his rights, he grew bitter, reckless, and faithless all at once.

In her disappointment and sorrow, longing for a friend, Aunt Debby entreated Miss Gale to come and stay with her. The governess had entered into possession of a morsel of money that sufficed for her moderate wants, and obviated the necessity of her teaching; so she came to Miss Debby for a visit, seemed like a sister, and so stayed on, until it became quite her home.

The change in fortune caused Aunt Debby to reduce the style of her housekeeping. The fashion of economy was this: all that in any way concerned P. was left as it had been, the reductions were such as would only touch Aunt Debby.

P. saw what was going on, and he did not object; it did not seem to him that he ought to be restricted; the world owed him something which he had not received—the other part of that million, you know.

Among the items with which Aunt Debby dispensed, we may reckon the invaluable Mrs. Jillet, first and foremost.

As had been mentioned by the metallic founder of the house of Dean, Mrs. Jillet had been somewhat exorbitant in the matter of wages; besides this, her office had had its perquisites, as what office has not? and Mrs. Jillet was prepared to retire from public life on a neat little competence.

Mrs. Jillet was not without a place of refuge; the excellent Mrs. Bently had found her services as a nurse falling into disrepute, on account of certain hints of inebriety; calls for her attendance became infrequent, and ceased altogether; and Mrs. Bently, who had with prudent forethought feathered her own nest, retired into it for safe-keeping—in other words, she opened a little public-house, called the Happy Home Hotel (Mrs. Bently pronounced it without the H's); in which 'Appy 'Ome there was a very small place for sleeping up stairs, and a very large place for drinking on the first floor.

To this 'Appy 'Ome, Mrs. Bently received Mrs. Jillet with effusion. Mrs. Jillet brought with her many elegant trappings, gathered from the superfluities of the house of Dean; she furnished a bedroom for herself, and mostly by daylight favored Mrs.

Bently with her society, in a little room opening off the bar, a tidy place, with the traditional red curtains, flaming carpet, and bunches of artificial flowers on the chimney piece. They were getting old, these women; they dyed their hair, wore caps and false teeth, and knew that by far the shorter part of their life journey lay before them; yet here they sat in the stuffy ante-room, gossipping together, conjointly dealing out poison to others; and as fate would have it, they sipped and sipped of the poison themselves.

When Aunt Debby had narrowed her expenditures to suit her income, she ventured to give her nephew a little advice.

"If you would go into business, my dear boy, you might soon have your money back again. Your fortune is not to be despised, and you might make a fine business on it. Your grandfather began with almost nothing, and you know how he succeeded."

"I don't know how to do anything," said P., "and I don't want to."

"Take a partner who does know."

"He'd cheat me; every one does. No; I shall not try business."

"Then, my dear boy, you ought really to live within your income. Consider that your whole property now is only about the income of two years."

"Well, then, I can live two years, or three, just as I have done, before it is all gone," said P., stubbornly.

"All gone! But, my dear, consider; you would beggar yourself."

"Maybe by that time I would be gone, too," said P.

"Don't speak so, my darling! It is not reasonable to think of your dying at four-and-twenty—a healthy fellow."

"Pshaw, Aunt Debby!" interrupted P. "If one finds the door locked, one can get out of the window, if necessary."

"O, my child, my child, you break my heart!" burst out Aunt Debby; and the poor old lady went off weeping, while all day long the echo of that pistol-shot, which had put her young brother out of this life, seemed to ring in her ears.

When Miss Gale sat down soberly to talk with her former pupil, telling him of all he might do and be, the calm wisdom of her words, the earnestness of her own purpose, the beauty of her own example, and perhaps a little of the old-time school-room respect, almost won him, and awoke in him the manhood which had been all these years smothered by pampering and idleness. If ever P. had been governed, taught self-restraint, responsibility, God-fearing, or man-fearing, or if he had inherited any grand moral purpose, this woman might have saved him; but all his life everything had been against him—ah! so cruelly and bitterly against him; there seemed not one bit of courage and moral strength, or ambition, left in him.

Moreover, the Devil was now ensnaring this poor boy most fatally with infidel literature. He had never had much religious training. Miss Debby had done something for him, and Miss Gale more. They had taught him Bible history; had taken him to church and given him a form of prayer; some good books, too, when he would read them. It had been but a poor grain-sowing, and a plentiful scattering of tares.

P. first ceased going to church on Sabbath mornings; and, from staying at home and reading novels, began to walk about the streets, take drives, and lounge into hotels. He did this to show himself a lad of spirit, because his associates jeered a little and coaxed a little. Next came the reading of evil books. It was singular that he who abhorred an argument for anything good, and could not follow a scientific discussion, perused with eagerness chapter after chapter of flimsy logic, pretending, and failing, to prove, that Nature was God, and Atheism was her prophet; that the Bible was a lie; religion a humbug; that the

Christ, who died and was sepulchred in Judea, had never a resurrection; that there is no incorruptible inheritance reserved for the sons of God. All these follies and blasphemies P. swallowed eagerly. It was not long before he felt learned enough in his new wisdom to set it forth in speech, and then how he horrified his poor aunt!

What! This boy whom she had taught to pray; this child by whose crib she had dreamed many a dream; this nephew who was to be her Christian gentleman embodied; was he telling her that her theology was an old woman's fable, and ranking the four holy Gospels with the ditties of Mother Goose? Aunt Debby tried to argue the matter. She was even more illogical than her boy, and failed signally to prove anything. She was right, but she contradicted herself a dozen times in as many sentences, and retreated ignominiously beaten, while that unfledged rascal held the field triumphant, shaking his head, looking belligerent, and daring all the world to conflict. Miss Gale did better with P., for she laughed at him, and told him he would outgrow his nonsense when he grew wiser, and know more both of men and science. She remarked to him that there was a "period of juvenescence, when lads take to infidelity as in yet earlier years they eat haws and rose-buds and chew spruce gum—all these little diversions grow equally distasteful as years pass by, and sense supersedes nonsense!"

How P. hated this fashion of dealing with his new creed! He was wild to prove to her that his assertions were the fruit of profound study, and a deep-rooted conviction. She only laughed the more, measured the time and the pages spent in this rare research, and remorselessly exhibited his ignorance, not to others, but to himself. She might have found her antidote sufficient for a cure, if there had been no meddling by quack doctors.

Our friend Roxwell had almost ceased to practise. He had grown rich, and liked to have leisure and to theorize. He was fond of coming in and talking to Aunt Debby for old times' sake—she was one of his few remaining patients. He heard all her troubles; was the confidante of all her anxieties. Chiefly she dwelt on her nephew's misfortunes and mischiefs.

"O, doctor, where can he have got such notions?"

"From Adam, I suppose," said the doctor, "where all our evil comes from. That unfortunate progenitor had a deal to answer for when he picked the apple; that fruit was a complete Pandora box of misfortunes to our race. Eating it, he filled all our veins with mischief; and Milton even accuses him of having, by the first bite, jogged earth's axis twenty-three and a half degrees; on account of which deviation, Miss Dean, you and I are nursing up our rheumatism over the register during the winter, and sweltering on our way to the mountains or the sea-side in the summer, in a vain effort to keep cool."

"Ah, doctor, how you do run on! But I wish you would try and see P., and reason with him," said Miss Dean.

"Look you here, my good friend," replied the doctor. "Do you know that reasoning would have more effect on our young man if long ago you had tried *ruling?* If he had been taught to obey, and had caught a sharp smack or two when he raised a general rumpus at the age of three or four, you might now reason. But what did you do in those days, Miss Dean? Why, you let him have his own way, or bribed him to get yours, which amounts to the same thing; so now he must even go on having his own way. It is a fact, madam, that those who are taught to respect and obey their parents, are the ones who will fear God and obey the laws of the land. You did a bad thing for P. when you let him come up in that Gilbert-go-gently fashion. He's out of your reach now; you can but look on,"

"I can and will keep on praying for him," sobbed Aunt Debby.

"Yes, yes; and it may save him. But what a pity that you did not preface your praying, or interline it, with a little active working! The praying alone would have done well enough if he had been out of your reach."

At this time P., miserably unsatisfied, went here and there, knowing the secret doors of gambling-hells, and the inside of dance-houses; a fast young man, poor fellow! trying to run away from the goadings of conscience and fierce unrest that pursued him, as the Furies pursued Orestes. Going everywhere, P. even strayed into Mrs. Bently's elysium of red curtains and stuffiness, the "Happy Home Hotel." Here he was received with enthusiasm, like a prince and a patron.

"Ah, Mr. Dean," said Mrs. Jillet, "there is no telling what feelings I have for you. I lived in that house and took care of it from your grandfather's time, and he *was* a hard gentleman to get along with; and I'd have willingly stopped there and died for the sake of all of you, if things hadn't happened just as they did. Me and Mrs. Bently often speaks of you; and if you ever want to drop in anywhere for hot gin and water to revive your spirits, we shall be more than pleased to give you a seat here, private."

"Yes, indeed we will," said Mrs. Bently, appearing with the refreshment named. "And more, sir, I was a-thinking as there might be times when you was out late, and for that and other reasons, didn't care for going home, for a small trifle of two or three dollars a week I'll engage always to have a room and a bed ready for you to come to.——Mrs. Jillet, dear, do look out of the window and see! there goes Mrs. Green in a black alapacca and a silk bonnet, and that little girl of hers set off in blue. She's quite coming out. If we called her in, and offered her a glass of gin, I'll warrant you, she'd be in the gutter, and the new clothes out at pawn, in a two-months. She's not strength of mind, like you and I have, poor thing!"

"No; that's true. I've a mind to call her," said Mrs. Jillet. And, opening the window, she leaned out between the red curtains, and bawled, "O, Mrs. Green! Can't you stop a minute, and speak to old friends?"

Mrs. Green shook her head, and moved on.

"O, but let me see your little girl. I am that fond of children!" said Mrs. Bently, leaning out by Mrs. Jillet. "What a dear she is! Do bring her in for a bit of candy, and you and I will have a drop of something warm, as we used to."

"No, no, no!" cried Mrs. Green, as if in terror, grasping her child's hand to pull her on.

"Ah!" shrieked Mrs. Jillet. "Mr. Dean wants to see you. He is in here—your own nurse-child—and would like to see them together as was every one of them a mother to his young days!"

P. saw his poor nurse hesitate; he felt he might be sitting there to lure her to a fall even more tremendous than the first; he remembered the homely breakfast at her house, and Teddy's honest satisfaction. He sprung up, oversetting his glass of hot gin and water, and, rushing out, met the woman and child on the doorstep.

"I don't want to see you, Mrs. Green—that is, not in there—I was only in of an errand—I'll walk along with you—are you going home?"—he rattled, flurried and blundering.

Mrs. Green drew a long breath. "It's no place for me—you came out, thank God! Well, that's the way He answered my prayer, 'Lead us not into temptation.' I did not know they lived there; and, please the Lord, I'll not walk on that square any more."

"No, don't. And don't let them call on you.

They are a pair of old witches. I heard them as good as say they wanted to destroy you. And there's Teddy, you know, and the little girl."

"And the last words of my old mother. She was buried a fortnight gone, sir." And Mrs. Green looked down at her black alpaca.

Meanwhile, Mrs. Jillet had said, "There! He's gone. They're both off. Well, there never was any doing anything with Mr. P. He's crochety."

"I hope he'll come again, and settle to have a lodging kept ready," said Mrs. Bently. "He would put many a penny in my pocket one way and another."

Indeed, P. did not reject Mrs. Bently's considerate offer. He thought it would be wonderfully convenient to have that out-of-the-way resort. He could not bear to go home and find Miss Gale quietly sitting up, book in hand. Nor was it any more agreeable to have Aunt Debby put her pale old face out of her door, her gray hair straying from under her night-cap, and to hear her say tremulously, "Good night, and God bless you, my dear boy!"

Good night! It was sure to be a bad night; for his head would whirl and buzz as his grand state bed danced *pirouettes* about his chamber, and one minute sailed up like a thistle-seed until he was bumped against the ceiling, and the next settled down, down, into the very cellar, and he felt the damp chill and feared the rats whose eyes gleamed at him out of the dimness of the wine-vaults. Ah, P. had very wearisome nights now! As he was undressing, he heard over and over again the sharp crack of the pistol that had sent his father uncalled, unprepared, unwelcome, into eternity. It was not the blues, such as succeeded juvenile parties; not the 'migraine,' such as had pre-empted part of his days at Saratoga, that attacked P. now. He was beginning to see little devils *couchant* in his bed-hangings, and queer creatures swung like tassels to his canopy.

Good night! P., when ever did you hear a good night, unless it was that one—your first on earth—when you slept on Aunt Debby's knees, and she cried over you, and over that still figure in the parlor, and the nurse and housekeeper gossipped over the misfortunes of "our family." After that night you were put to sleep on gin-sling, and Universal Baby Panacea, and you ate too much, and dreamed dreams which there was no Joseph to interpret, and you could not rest because you could not work, and we know that Ann told you ghost-stories,—now you are going to bed to hear strange noises, to see horrible sights, to take mysterious excursions from basement to attic, and Aunt Debby says "Good night!" As for the other part, the tremulous "God bless you!" why, P., that is all nonsense to your wise ear; for you are quite satisfied that there is no God; that there is nothing higher and better than your feeble, wine-fettered thought can reach!

P. was still a favorite in society; he was rather fast, the good people admitted, but he would moderate his rate of speed some day, and go more slowly to destruction. He was a young gentleman of leisure; he had some wealthy relatives, cousins and uncles, on his mother's side; he had the hundred thousand dollars which his administrators had not had time to use up, and people expected him to get something from Aunt Debby, who, it was brilliantly remarked, "could not live for ever." The paternal Snell was not the only person who had a spare daughter or two from whom P. could select a wife. P. was inclined to quarrel with Snell about business; but Snell reasoned mildly with him: "My dear fellow, did I not tell you that the whole matter rested with Pincham? *I* could not interfere with him. I do not like the look of matters now, I must say, but I had confidence in Pincham; why, he had a brother whose honesty was a proverb all over the city. Who would think that an honest man's brother would be dishonest?"

So in one way and another, by fair words, good dinners, pleasant parties, warm welcomes, and plenty of flattery, Snell, Esq., coaxed P. back to his house. The boy was young and soft, heart-sick and lonesome, to tell the truth. He began to think Evelina Snell very pretty; she had blue eyes, yellow curls, and the slenderest waist in the world. P. thought that was beauty.

Our young friend liked to call on Evelina; to dance with her. He paid her so much attention, that father Snell began to give odious little winks when he saw the two together, and to remark to mamma Snell that P. was a good sort of fellow, and his house was very stylish, and likely Miss Debby Dean had a neat sum to tie up.

CHAPTER TENTH.

P. reaches a Crisis.

"Into this world we come, like ships
Launched from the docks, and stocks, and slips,
For fortune fair or fatal."

CHAPTER TENTH.

P. reaches a Crisis.

IT is quite the style for young men to join some club association. P. must be in the fashion, and joined one. There are many of these organizations which might have been recommended to him; certain "Sons," and "Knights Templar," and "Good Templars," and so on, would have lent a hand to drag him up out of the quicksands into which he was slowly sliding. P. joined none of these. If he had gone over to the "Young Men's Christian Association," there might have been a rescue for him, and we should have been saved writing this history for a warning. Instead, P. joined the R. B's. *R. B.* might mean "Royal Brothers," "Roaring Blades," or "Rowdy Boys," for aught I know—not having joined the R. B.'s, one cannot tell what the cabalistic letters mean. The R. B.'s had a fine room, luxuriously furnished: sofas and chairs were gorgeous in red velvet; the lace curtains were all beautiful with lilies and roses, and sprays of fern, and heads of wheat, white and delicate as sea-foam;

grand chandeliers, with gilded chains, and glittering pendants, hung over marble tables, and mosaic tables, and tables for billiards, cards, checkers, and dice—any game in fact, good or evil, that could amuse. The R. B.'s had servants and wine; they ate, drank, and were merry. P. was quite fascinated with them; he thought he had at last found something to interest him, something congenial; they drank his favorite drinks; sang the jolliest songs; were so witty; so wise. They did not believe these hobgoblin tales of immortal spirits; of a Day of Judgment; of Heaven and Hell; of a Creator and a Judge. The R. B.'s all knew better; and P. was glad to be in their truly choice and refined company.

He was away from home so constantly, out so late, or all night, when he went to Mrs. Bently's "Happy Home," that Aunt Debby ventured to inquire what was being done. She was told that he had joined a "Literary Society."

"That is very nice," said the simple old lady. "You hear, Miss Gale, it is a literary society to which P. belongs. I always knew there was more in him than people thought."

Yes, there was doubtless plenty in P., but nobody had ever taken well-concerted measures for bringing it out.

As for Miss Gale, she was suspicious of the literary attainments and pursuits of P.'s literary confreres. She judged that they were better acquainted with "Hoyle on Games" than with "Edwards on the Will;" that they preferred choice Burgundy to Lord Maccaulay; and took more kindly to *rouge-et-noir* than to the "Testimony of the Rocks."

For all their elegance and their abundant refreshments our young R. B.'s had to pay heavily. P. was making his money fly in royal fashion. His friends hinted, or plainly remonstrated, but the young man replied that he thought the cash would hold out as long as he wanted it; and indeed, Aunt Debby helped the holding out, by seeing to it that P. was never at any expense at home, and by paying every bill that came to her knowledge.

Among the chief expenses of the R. B. club, or society, might be counted an annual dinner, on what they called their anniversary. This dinner was given in magnificent style at a first-class hotel, and to it they invited their particular friends. Previous to the dinner they had songs and speeches at their society-room, and then drove about town in open carriages, wearing badges, and striving to attract attention.

A hundred years ago, courtly and cultivated gentlemen thought it no particular disgrace to drink themselves under the table. The R. B.'s took the same view; they would have branded him a poltroon who was afraid to drink freely, and they had no idea of blushing when they became drunk. Hitherto P. had never publicly disgraced himself, nor occasioned any severe remarks; it had been hinted that he was fond of a glass of wine, and that if he did not have a care he might soon drink too much. Teddy had found him unable to take care of himself; Miss Gale and Aunt Debby had looked anxiously after his unsteady steps as he went to his bed; we remember that a policeman had found him sitting on a curbstone, hilarious and ridiculous, but that matter had been hushed up, and society still spoke well of Mr. P. Dean, and had never had occasion to point at him the finger of scorn.

P. was now rapidly passing the bounds of prudence; he was reckless of consequences, careless of condemnation. At the R. B.'s dinner P. was in his element. He was one of the masters of ceremonies, and having performed his part to every one's satisfaction until wine was set on the table, he began to drink greedily. The long table was closely surrounded by young men. Large bouquets and beautiful wreaths glowed over the whiteness of the damask table linen; and down the whole length of the festive board decanters cast crimson or golden reflections as the light streamed through them; bottles of what was called choice wine stood singly or in groups; fragile crystal glasses; elegant goblets, cut with a tracery of leaves and flowers, sparkled almost as bright as the silverware that was abundantly displayed; while a grand mirror, at the lower extremity of the table, caught up and reduplicated the brilliant scene in its shining depths. Near the upper door of the apartment sat the band that had been engaged to furnish music for the occasion, and servers of wine and brandy were sent betimes to the performers.

The merriment grew furious; several toasts would be shouted forth at once; faces were flushed; eyes gleaming; some overcome already were nodding drowsily in their chairs, heedless of the bacchanalian din. A madness seized P. He had become furiously drunk. He caught an uncorked bottle of champagne in one hand and a decanter of brandy in the other, and vaulted upon the table with a wild huzza. His inebriated companions broke into cheers and laughter. P. crashed the bottle and decanter together in an ecstasy, and the wine, set free, spirted and foamed into his face, and over the splendors of his apparel. Laughter now filled the room, and some cried, "Come down, come down; none of that!"

But the distracted Dean had now caught sight of himself in the long mirror; he was too drunk to recognise his own semblance, and frantically imagined that here was some enemy mocking him with absurd gestures. Full of wrath, he stooped down, and, grasping whatever bottles and glasses came to hand, flung them crashing through the mocking mirror. Waiters rushed to the rescue, but were prevented from seizing P. by the crowd shouting and gesticulating, upbraiding and laughing about the table, making ineffectual efforts to grasp P.'s active legs and pull him down.

The very demon of destruction was rampant in this young man; he dexterously seized bottles, and struck at the heads of his assailants; he kicked the ornamental silverware right and left; he made a clean sweep of one end of the table by an agile use of his right leg, and dashed glass and silver, liquids and solids, on the floor. For a few minutes the room was full of cries and oaths and the crash of breaking glass. The waiters, the landlord, and the loungers in the bar-room ran to look; the band dropped their instruments, and yelled with laughter. P. was caught by head, arms, and legs, and, dragged from the table, was held extended among his captors, still denouncing the man who had gibed and flouted at him in the mirror. Ignominiously was the master of ceremonies carried to a small upper room, and put to bed, there to recover his senses, remember, and be ashamed. The anniversary dinner broke up in confusion, and all night the hotel servants were busy repairing damages.

The third day after this the irate landlord sent P. a bill of eleven hundred dollars for damages. This P. walked down and paid without a murmur, but by this restitution he could not check the current of remark and scandal. Every one was talking against him: those who had fostered the love of drink in him, those who had evoked the demon in the innocent boy, now held up their hands in horror and protested at his drunkenness. P. knew very well why Aunt Debby fell ill and kept her bed for a week, but Miss Gale never said why; she met him on the same good terms as ever, pitying the poor young sinner with all her heart, and feeling that this was not the time for upbraiding. Perhaps P.'s heart was a little softened by her wise kindness, for he hung about her and grew more confidential, refraining also from all remarks that were displeasing to her. Neither did Evelina Snell berate him: Evelina cried a little when she first heard of the fracas, cried not because P. had done wrong, and was in danger of doing even worse, but because she feared people would laugh at him, and say unpleasant things of her.

Miss Gale and Teddy Green tried more than ever to get P. to go into business; so did Dr. Roxwell. They suggested country life, a farm with a nice residence, and an overseer hired to look after the work; they proposed a long trip overland with some one experienced in buying furs; they offered to get him a chance to go with an exploring expedition; they recommended a partnership in a lumber business, and that P. should go up into Maine for awhile, but the young man sullenly and decidedly rejected all advice.

P. had sinned grievously, and society made him know it, by averted looks and caustic speeches.

The "R. B.'s" felt their honorable clique disgraced by the frantic interruption of their dinner, and though P. had paid damages, they ignominiously expelled him from their number, a circumstance which might have been of great advantage to the victim if he had only known how to use it. But being deprived of the companionship of the brilliant "R. B.'s," he spent most of his evenings playing billiards in a saloon with a "bar" attached to it, where he partook freely of brandy and water. In one way and another P. contrived to lose a little money here, and losing made him cross. He had the diversion of growling and disputing every evening, and on one unlucky occasion he doubled up his fists and shook them in his opponent's face. "Ah, ha!" said that person, aggravatingly, "do you take me for that fellow you saw in the glass at the R. B. dinner? You mashed his head with a decanter, you know, and what did it cost you?"

By way of reply to this taunt, P. knocked the speaker down, but he sprung up again in a second, and gave P. a black eye. The combatants were parted presently, and P., feeling quite unfit to go home, his eye being bruised and his coat torn, concluded to put into Mrs. Bently's "'Appy 'Ome 'Otel" for repairs. Just as he reached the door, the fellow with whom he had quarrelled came after him, and renewed the attack.

In the light of the street gas, and the red light which came through the windows of Mrs. Bently's sanctum, P. went into the quarrel in such loud earnest that a policeman came up to stop the fight. The one rioter fled incontinently, but P. having lost his last morsel of sense, pulled out a mite of a revolver, which looked about as terrible as a pea-shooter, and fired one impotent shot at the policeman's head; he went so wide of the mark that the bit of a ball flew through Mrs. Bently's sign, and P., being seized, was the second time locked up by the police, but now on charge of "riotous conduct, and violent assault of an officer."

When P. came to his senses, next morning, he cursed his unhappy stars, as if the planets had anything to do with getting him into disgrace.

Teddy Green had now advanced to the position of newspaper reporter; Teddy had studied hard, and had made bold to imitate Benjamin Franklin, and contribute small articles to the paper on which he worked. He had grown in favor, and was climbing upwards at a very moderate rate, having only his own honest endeavors to look to.

Teddy going about the city for last *items* for his paper, had learned of P.'s misconduct, and its consequences. We may be sure that Teddy did not seize the bit of scandal, to make an amusing paragraph of it as a relish for the breakfast of those two unfortunate women, Aunt Debby and Miss Gale. Instead, he sent a note to the ex-governess, telling her the cause of P.'s absence, and where he might be found, if he were looked after.

Miss Gale went for Dr. Roxwell to help her in the trouble, for she knew that the doctor was one of her reckless boy's best friends.

The two found P. in a dismal little room, having a

small iron bedstead with dirty covers, and a rickety table. On the table stood a bowl of porridge and molasses, with a battered iron spoon stuck up in the middle. It is needless to say that P. had utterly contemned this poor fare, and he now lay on the pallet, his face to the wall; his muddy boots kicked off; his hair uncombed; his face unwashed, and marred by last evening's strife; his coat torn; his shirt-front rent; his necktie vanished; his watch, chain, ring, and pocket-book put somewhere for safe-keeping by his captors.

"Well, well, well!" said Dr. Roxwell, and his mind made a hasty review of this young man's life; the splendor of his early prospects; the luxurious indulgence; he could see as in a picture the babe with three nurses, in his grand nursery, or taking a state progress through the streets. Aunt Debby's petted boy, dressed in velvets, giving juvenile parties, and assisted on in learning and in life by every tender device for saving him trouble, and giving him his own way. "Well, well, well!" said the doctor again.

"O, P., my dear P.! how sorry I am for you! We must get you out of this and take you home, and try and do better, all of us!" cried Miss Gale.

"I won't go home," said the dishevelled P., sulkily.

"Ah! now, no one knows a word of this; it is

not in the papers, and won't be. Teddy Green let us hear of it; he is such a good fellow. If you don't like to go home, we will go out in the country to see my uncle; I'd like it so well. Sit up, P.; do, now, and the doctor will try and settle your business over at the court, and bring us a hack to go home in."

"I wish he'd been to my funeral yesterday, instead of his cousin Nancy's," said P., morbidly.

"You must not say *that*, my boy. I tell you you are far from being ready to die."

"Being ready to die is all bosh," said P., defiantly.

"No, it is not," said Miss Gale, "you know better. You feel in your own heart that you are more than a dog or a bird to drop dead and be nothing evermore. And you know just as well that you'd be perfectly wretched in Heaven if you were taken there this minute just as you are, for you don't like good things, and don't love God. My dear fellow, to live is the very best thing that can befall you, and you have only to try and get some comfort out of that estate. Why, boy, the world lies before you. You have yet money, and friends, and health; and you can make more according to your wish, if you'll set about it. Come, P., you must turn over a new leaf and reform; get a nice wife to make home lively and homelike to you, and be a man. This is a sad tumble, but pick yourself up, and be a man hereafter. When you were a little fellow you could do anything you put your mind to."

Dr. Roxwell had gone out on his errand, feeling himself quite overcome by P.'s forlorn condition.

Miss Gale had pulled her former pupil from his crouching by the wall as she spoke, and now he lay with his head on the dirty straw pillow, looking up into her face, as she bent over him, pitying, reproving, encouraging. He caught the ends of her shawl, and hid his face in them, sobbing out: "O, I wish I were a little boy in the school-room with you again; and that I could come up to live better and be happy."

"You can live better and be happy all the same," said Miss Gale, as her tears dropped on his rumpled hair, while she smothered it with her hand. "You must settle to some work, so you will not be tempted by idleness to go to these places where you get into so much trouble. It is unmanly, my dear P., to live without any motive, and without any good result. Life is for honest effort, and for fair success, not for a general row. You are capable of something far better than you have yet sought after. I say it, P., who have known it since you were five years old."

"It's no use," moaned P. "I'm always coming to grief. I get to those places, and there's an end of me. Why are people allowed to have traps to catch us poor weak fellows in every turn of the street? I can't do any better, and there is no use talking!"

"You can do better, my dear fellow, if you begin in the right way," said Miss Gale, sitting down on the edge of the bed and looking earnestly at P. "A man can make no progress in goodness when he reviles and rejects the Fountain of all goodness. 'Every good and every perfect gift is from above, and cometh down from the Father of Lights;' and you, my poor boy, even deny his existence. I should think, P., that the known evil of your own heart, the manner in which you sin and are sinned against, would convince you of an adversary to your goodness and happiness, stronger than you can conquer. But you see, P., that all men do not sin and fall and suffer as you do. There are many that shine in virtue and in peace; whose lives are blessed and a blessing, whom we all love and honor perforce. This is not because they are naturally better or stronger or wiser than you; but because they have gotten help where you have scorned it; because they have obeyed the commands of a Master and Father, whom you ignore to your own destruction. Take the right means, my P., and you will secure the desired end. Cease this vain babbling of infidelity; submit to God, and he will raise you up. All life is before you; everything good is possible to you. You can rise superior to all these downfalls and temptations. They talk of wild oats, P.—I think you have sowed and harvested of them pretty plentiful'y already."

P.'s hard short sobs had ceased; he listened attentively.

"When I talk to you, and hear you," he said, "it seems as if I could be something and do right. Then in a little time the feeling is gone, and I am in trouble as before."

"But now you will truly try and do better; try in the right way, will you not?"

"Yes, I will try," said P.

Then he got up from the horrible pallet; put on his boots; left his coat for the warden or the next comer; put on the spring overcoat which the doctor had brought him; fastened up his necktie; straightened his cap, and crushed it over his shaggy hair and black eye, and began tramping uneasily up and down the narrow limits of his cell; while Miss Gale sat on the edge of the bed, recalling the past as the doctor had recalled it; sympathizing with the present; trembling for the future; wondering if her boy would now reform.

At home, Aunt Debby cried softly over her prayers and her Bible, and wondered if it were at all her fault that P. had reached this crisis in his history.

CHAPTER ELEVENTH.

Police Court to the Rescue.

"Of letting loose rapine and murder,
To go *just so far and no further;*
And setting all the land on fire,
To burn just so high, *and no higher.*"

CHAPTER ELEVENTH.

Police Court to the Rescue.

P HAD said that "he would try"—we cannot tell whether he kept his promise or not; if he did, his keeping was of poor fashion enough. Perhaps by this time he was incapable of strong effort, or high resolution. Moral purpose in P. had been probably still-born; surely it had never been fostered, and taught, and equipped to be a captain over the spiritual being, leading obedient powers to grand conquest. P.'s faculties were disorganized and demoralized; and his trying was like the last feeble flutter of the singed moth, fallen dying out of the flame.

Dr. Roxwell wanted to know who was responsible for this. Was P. to blame for not having been dowered with virtues before his birth? for having been left so wretchedly untrained? Was he to blame for finding himself now too weak to resist temptation, and too blind to discern clearly between good and evil?

"Who hath sinned, this man or his parents? That is what I want to know; and by parents I mean all these people who have had charge of him—nurses and servants, guardians, Aunt Debby, and Professor Easy, with the other teachers. Dear me! who can be to blame among all of them?"

Thus spoke Dr. Roxwell, addressing his cousin Nancy's tombstone. The loss of Cousin Nancy fell heavily on the doctor; she had been such an admirable listener, that her like would never be found again.

"Business!" said P., when some sort of occupation was urged upon him. "What business can *I* do? I can't open a hotel?"

"Shocking! No; of course not," said Aunt Debby

"And grandfather and father were liquor-dealers; but I don't know as I could undertake the business."

"By no means; it would be the ruin of you!" cried Miss Gale.

"Past spoiling, by this time," said P., indifferently. "Well, I have no profession, and I've never been used to study or thinking, or talking. I cannot set up as a politician."

"There are other things to turn to—farming," said Miss Gale.

"Farming! I hate the country, and should die of a quiet life."

"It would be free from temptations which are fatal to you."

"Ah! but I believe I like the temptations," said P., perversely.

"Manufactures—commerce—stores of all kinds," said Aunt Debby.

"Don't bother me," said P. "I can't do anything. Don't you know, Aunt Debby, I was never brought up to do anything. The maid laced my shoes; the waiter spread my bread, and put my egg into the cup, when I was twelve years old; and you did my sums, Aunt Debby, if Miss Gale set me hard ones; and yet I do believe I should have liked books and study, if I had been allowed a chance. Lo! the work of your hands!"

This was very bitter to Aunt Debby. She began to see dimly the folly, and even sin, of her management of her nephew. We have dreamed dreams of standing on a narrowing space, and seeing two great walls drawing together from either side, to crush us. So Aunt Debby saw now looming up on the one hand the errors and mismanagement of P.'s childhood, and on the other, the dim foreshadowing of their dire effect. These things were crushing her poor well meaning old heart.

"P.," said Miss Gale, "what is going to be done to save you? You are on the verge of ruin."

"Just toppling over," admitted P.

"Then, how *can* we help you?"

"There is no way," said P. "If there were any strong power to take hold of me, to threaten me with a knife to my throat, and resolutely kill or cure me, the problem of my existence would be solved, somehow, immediately. Sometimes I think of what I used to read in history of the code of Draco, and the iron laws of Lycurgus, when a man's daily living was looked after, and a man's crime against himself was a crime against the state and visited accordingly, and I wish I had lived under such a government."

"Would you like to be a mere puppet, and shift all responsibility for your own actions?"

"If one has ceased to be a responsible agent, it is well to be taken care of. I shall go out by-and-by—I shall pass an open door, where I shall see fellows that I know, laughing and drinking and beckoning—I shall see the liquor that plays the mischief with me—I shall smell it—I shall go in and drink it, and I cannot tell you whether I shall get home safely, or whether I shall come to grief, and be brought up in a station-house, or whether I shall die out somewhere, like a spark of fire in the darkness, and never be heard of any more."

"O, how can you talk so? how can you do so?" cried Miss Gale.

"The trouble is that the shop is open, and the fellows are there, and the liquor is there. Suppose I walked through all the city, and did not find one groggery, one wholesale or retail liquor-store, one bar, one place at all where liquors were sold? If I could absolutely get nothing stronger than Saratoga water, lemonade, or the nectar out of a soda-fountain, you might see me coming home early, safe and sound; getting more of a man every day, and capable of doing something by-and-by. If it had been so since I was born, I would not be lying here now, as nearly ruined as can be without being gone altogether."

P. got up, and lounged out of the room.

"O, for a strong, well-maintained prohibitory law!" cried Miss Gale.

"My dear," suggested Aunt Debby, "we do not want tyrannical laws to make slaves of us—we are a free people."

"We could not be made slaves by a law made by ourselves, for our own protection," said Miss Gale.

"But it seems that we have no right to legislate what a man shall eat and drink. Has he not a right to put into his mouth whatever he pleases?"

"No," said the governess. "It is right to control everything for the greatest good of the greatest number, and attain the highest happiness. We assert the right to frame laws forbidding the sale of poisons, except to responsible parties for a known and legitimate use: the law is often evaded; parties are deceived; but it is there, and should be enforced to the very letter. We know it is a just and proper law; and the greatest evil-working, soul-and-body-destroying poison of all, is sold openly by the barrel, and people cry out that it would not be just to forbid its manufacture and its sale."

"Ah, yes. But, after all, it is not like laudanum, prussic acid, or strychnine," said Aunt Debby.

"It takes a good deal to do the work that a small portion of those poisons will effect—it is slower in its working, but, after all, not less painful. People suffer a drunkard's death a thousand times before he dies; he breaks the hearts of his family for years. It would be less cruel if he were killed at once by the poison, if he must only die by it after all."

"I'm just as anxious for P. as you are. I'd give my life to see him reformed. God knows, Miss Gale,

I would willingly have died for that boy, any day since he was born; my days have not so very much good left in them that I should desire their prolongation. But when we get talking of this temperance question, do you know I get all mixed up. It is so different from anything that I was brought up to. In my young days even ministers drank both wine and whiskey, and no harm was thought of it."

"Yes," said Dr. Roxwell, who had walked in. "They primed for the pulpit, possibly, with a good glass of brandy; and some of them are now opposed to total abstinence. I think very many of those who drank as they pleased twenty, thirty, fifty years since, would *now* go in for absolute prohibition, because they see the effects of the example on the mass, and the horrible and spreading evils of intemperance."

"If it was a sin then, it is a sin now," said Aunt Debby; "and I have always heard temperance people called fanatics."

"Some of them are fanatics, having more zeal in their hearts than knowledge in their heads, and so bring the cause into disrepute—but it is safest to err on the right side. Moreover, most of the agitators of the temperance question are gentlemen and scholars, whole-hearted philanthropists, and worthy of our grateful support. When one claims that the use of wine or liquor is a sin, per se, one makes a claim that cannot be logically proved or supported, and presently runs into fanaticism."

"And some say it is wrong to use wine in the Sacrament."

"Then they say what they have no right to say—I don't believe—yes, I am sure that it is impossible that it can be proven that the wine tasted at the communion-table ever caused or re-aroused the craving for strong drink; and, at all events, when Christ without doubt did take wine and bread, and dividing it, say, 'This do,' I, for one, shall be perfectly content to do it, and feel that I am doing right."

"And how about the wine and brandy in medicine prescribed by physicians?" asked Miss Gale.

"I don't use it, for fear of doing more harm than good; though I have had a plenty of patients with whom I would have been perfectly safe in prescribing it. It takes us a long while to learn physical facts, Miss Gale, and we are ever making new discoveries in medicine. I have a very ancient medical book, which instructs us how to cure idiots, by rubbing the head with an oil made out of a man's skull and other ingredients. I need not tell you we do not now deal with idiocy in that fashion. Maybe, a hundred years from now, some of our present prescriptions may have become obsolete."

Still, as they talked at home, P., the object of their cares and fears, wandered on his way, and found a net spread at the head of every street, to take the sons of the nation, as Isaiah saw in vision.

"The law," says St. Paul, "is holy, and the commandment is holy, just, and good." He was speaking of the law and commandment of our God, and not of men; for the civil law is given to calling good evil, and evil good; or, in other words, what is evil may become good by payment of certain dollars and cents; what is lawful as a cause, is criminal as an effect.

To murder your neighbor is a capital crime; nevertheless, you may murder your neighbor in a perfectly legal manner, if you pay, say twenty dollars for a license, and proceed to the deed in a sufficiently leisurely manner. You cannot cut off A. B. in the prime of his days with a dose of strychnine, and be uncondemned. The state cries out for vengeance on the destroyer. The state, at heavy cost, tries, condemns, and executes you. And yet, if you pay the state your twenty dollars, you may sell A. B. two hundred dollars' worth of strychnine whiskey, which shall so madden him that he will first cut his wife's throat and then his own. The state will then raise no lamentations for him; he will be pronounced a fool who did not know the limit of his strength, and a villain whom society is well rid of. Meanwhile, if you have dealt with C. and D., and all the rest of the alphabet, as you did with A. B., and have made enough by the operation to ride in a carriage, and give election treats, you may reasonably look forward to going to Congress, to help frame laws which shall make your murder-license cheaper, and your whiskey-profits heavier.

Licenses and liquor-taxes are a source of emolument to the Government; fires, thefts, murders, and trials in courts, big and little, are an expense to the state; the latter would more than overbalance the former; if people would take the trouble to consider, it would be seen that the liquor trade is a source of impoverishment rather than of gain, and beyond the money loss we must set the loss of men. Rachel is bereaved of her children.

The unfortunate young man whose history we chronicle had now reached a point where he grew reckless of opinions, and careless of disgrace. He belonged to a class in society whose faults have frequently been overlooked, and who have supposed that, through courtesy, they should escape punishment; whereas, on the principle that where "much is given, much shall be required," they merit additional severity, because they have had unusual opportunity; the influence of their bad example is greater; the debt they owe society is heavier P.'s errors could no longer be ignored, and his appearances in the police court were frequent. As in days gone by they dealt with the maniac with stripes and chains and foul dungeons, now they deal with the rum maniac with fines and imprisonment; and there is just as much likelihood of success in the one case as in the other.

The fines and imprisonment are just what is needed, applied in the right quarter; for instance, to the maker and vender of liquors that intoxicate. When you get to the drunkard, you find a man sick in body and *non compos mentis*, and you must heal, and not punish. The magistrate should know of some hospital for drunkards, some infirmary for topers, some madhouse for delirium tremens, and have power to send his culprit there for the right kind of treatment.

"We're a 'avin' werry good times just now," says little Mollie O'Shane. "Mammy's been in the 'Ouse of Correction for three week, an' daddy was only out a week when he got shut up agin, an' we 'as werry good times, Pat an' me."

If said "daddy" had been where he could have

been given medical treatment, instead of an absurd imprisonment, the disgrace and confinement of which made not the slightest impression on Mr. O'Shane's blunted sensibilities, Mollie and her wee brother might have seen even better days yet.

We leave you to consider what sort of an appetizer such a paragraph as this in the morning paper proved to Aunt Debby and Miss Gale:—

"Before Alderman Beitler, for drunkenness, P. Dean; fined five dollars and costs."

"Officer Murphy yesterday evening arrested P. Dean, and a young man, name unknown, on charge of drunkenness and riotous conduct."

"A riot of a serious character took place on Monday evening at a tavern kept on Water street by Mrs. Bently. A young man, named P. Dean, belonging to one of the first families in the city—a millionaire, says report—struck an old man on the head with a bottle of Rocky Mountain Bitters. The injury was quite severe, and the wounded man was taken to the hospital. Dean was brought before Justice Norton, and gave bail for his appearance when called for."

In one year P. spent three weeks—all days and parts of days being counted—in jail. He paid three hundred and sixty-nine dollars for fines and damages; his name appeared fourteen times in the police columns of the city papers; he was at different times days in bed, amounting to four weeks, recovering from injuries received in drunken brawls; he lost two front teeth, and had a scar across his chin, tokens not of valor but of whiskey bouts; he paid Mrs. Bently five hundred dollars for bed, board, attendance, and hush-money—a sum, she assured him, much below her true bill, but the reduction "was on account of her devoted affection for, and undying interest in, a young man to whom she had been as a mother."

"My dear boy," said Miss Gale, sitting by the bed where P. lay, with his head bound up. "You speak of the law; I am sure it has taken you in hand, and I cannot see that you are at all benefited."

"No," sighed P. "There's a screw loose somewhere."

"This fining and imprisoning drunkards is all bosh," said Dr. Roxwell, from his station at the window. "The disgrace is nothing; they don't care for it; and you might as well talk of shutting a lunatic up fourteen days for his lunacy, or fining a madman five dollars for being mad. You've got to take hold of drunkards another way entirely."

"I'll tell you whom they ought to fine," cried P., sitting up in bed.

"My dear P., do lie down," remonstrated Miss Gale.

"They ought to fine that old hag, Bently, who makes the drunkards with her 'Rocky Mountain Cordial,' and 'Mountain Bitters.' They ought to fine her so heavily that she'd have to sell out the whole concern to pay it."

P. gesticulated wildly with his fists; and Miss Gale entreated, "Oh! P., my dear, do control yourself, and lie down."

"I'll tell you who ought to go to prison—yes, for life—Curdle & Sons, importers of wines and brandies. I'll tell you where the law should interfere—with Maxwell Brothers, wholesale and retail liquor-dealers; half a million they're worth, and government should confiscate the whole of it. Who is it they should haul up in court and reprimand, and disgrace, and all that? Why, it is Langley, with that accursed first-class bar in his hotel; and Pingle with his grand saloon; and Huxford, with his 'Metropolitan Retreat.'"

"Yes; that's the truth, P.," said Dr. Roxwell. "But you'd better lie down, and think no more about it."

"I *will* think about it. These liquor-sellers, like so many——"

"P., you will certainly be worse," urged Miss Gale.

"I'd be glad to be dead," vociferated P.——"like so many highwaymen, attack me, plunder me, leave me half dead, and up steps the wisdom of the law, and fines me for obstructing the public way with my maimed and insensible carcass. I'm robbed by Pingle, and Huxford, and the Maxwell Brothers, and the Court sends me to jail for not taking better care of my money. Here's a man pays thirty dollars for his license to sell, but I can't get any license to drink. Ah ha! They know I'll drink without a license, and be fined for it, and go to the lock-up for it—so the state imagines it makes money out of both of us, buyer and seller; but when you come to foot up the bills, and the expenses for trials, and for courts, and for injury to public property, and support of public institutions, why, you'll see that the state has been penny wise and pound foolish; it has been gaining by tens and losing by thousands, by jingo!"—and the unhappy orator flounced himself over, buried his bandaged head in a corner by the wall, and jerked the bed-clothes into an uncomfortable pile.

"Doctor," said Miss Gale, "I'm afraid the poor fellow has gone crazy."

"That is the most sensible speech he has ever made; pity that he won't profit by his own wisdom," said the doctor, gruffly.

Here came in Aunt Debby, who had been making ineffectual efforts to get a nap. No longer the comely lady who superintended the baby heir's morning bath, or, gracious and lovely, received her callers on New Year's Day; but a haggard woman, with deep-set, tear-blinded eyes; wrinkles cut down into her face like watercourses; a sharp chin, its rounded prettiness worn away long ago; a nose like an eagle's beak, and thin hair, white as snow.

"Didn't I hear my poor child speaking?" asked Aunt Debby, drawing her shawl about her thin, bent shoulders, and stepping very feebly. "O, my poor love, what can help him!"

"Nothing, I fear," said Dr. Roxwell. "There is no help in us selfish sinners, and he won't look higher up."

CHAPTER TWELFTH.

The Asylum Undertakes Him.

"Heavy to get, and hard to hold,
Hoarded, bartered, bought and sold,
Stolen, borrowed, squandered, doled,
Spurned by the young, and hugged by the old
To the very edge of the churchyard mould."

CHAPTER TWELFTH.

The Asylum undertakes P.

EVER impending over the inebriate is the drunkard's horrible delirium—*mania à potu.* P. had seen the bed going up and down—he had seen queer creatures swinging in hideous sport to his bed's canopy; he had shrunk from the eyes of rats that gleamed on him from grim corners—but feeling, fearing, and shrinking, he had known that these were only fancies, one part of the brain had reasoned, while the other imagined, and P. had borne up against these horrors.

P.'s conduct had of late been such that the paternal Snell had withdrawn patronage from him; had ceased winking and hinting, and had very nearly concluded that a marriage between P. and Evelina was not to be thought of, because it was evident that the last hundred thousand out of that million was rapidly melting away.

Poor P. had given Evelina his picture, and she had

promised him hers in return. He called one evening to get it.

"Pa says I can't give it to you," said Evelina, reluctantly.

"Can't! why not?" demanded P.; "what's up, now?"

"It's all your own fault, P.," whimpered Evelina; "you are not behaving right—you will get into such disgraceful trouble. People say you drink too much, P.—why will you? You see it is all your own fault that Pa won't let me give it to you."

Evelina was growing incoherent, and P. shouted, angrily,—

"*My* fault! it's *their* fault. Your father gave me drink plenty of times; offered it to me; forced it on me. So did your mother—so did *you.*"

"Ah, but everybody likes a *little;* the trouble with you is, that you take too much."

"Much, and little, is it? Who is going to find out what is much and what is little? Little for one, is much for another, and when a fellow gets going he don't know where to stop, and everybody begins to drop down on him."

Evelina, weeping, assured P. that she did not wish to drop down on him in this offensive manner; on the contrary, the unhappy Evelina was ready to stand by

P., and let people drop down on both of them, if people were so cruel.

"I'm just what all of you folks, and everybody else, have been making of me ever since I was born," said P., sulkily; "and everybody turns against me, and *you* turn against me; and, confound it all! I'll go and hang myself, and be done with it."

"I don't turn against you," sobbed Evelina, "and I never will. You must not talk of hanging yourself—don't, P., don't do it; say you won't—promise me."

"Will you promise me you'll marry me?" asked P.

"Well—yes—I will; only I don't know what pa 'll say."

"And where's that picture?" demanded P., pushing his advantage.

"It's in my pocket," said Evelina, slowly producing it.

"Give it to me, then," said P., taking it without any great ardor; "and to-morrow I'll bring you a ring, and we'll see what your father will say. It is a poor time for him to turn against me, after all his encouragement, and I won't stand it."

P. was grumbling at Snell, instead of going into any raptures over Evelina and the promise she had just made him. He was not very lover-like, and the poor child felt it. She had no undying devotion for P., not a particle of respect for him; the fancy which his attentions and her parent's hints had fostered, she called love. It was but a poor, faint shadow of a grand emotion; but it was all Evelina knew, and she was ready to cry that P. should be occupied in quarrelling against her father, rather than saying fond words to her.

"Pa won't object, P., if—if you will only be careful. You must not drink so much, not enough to get into trouble. Say you give it up, P., and go into business; I think it would be so nice. Can't you have a fine store, like young Curtis?"

"I'm not up to that sort of thing," replied P.

"And about the other, why, say you'll be careful, and not drink so much."

"Confound it!" cried P., "I guess I know how to take care of myself. You never mind, Evelina—there, now, what are you crying for? Yes, I'll be careful after this; will that suit you?"

Evelina wiped her eyes, and smiled. "What will your Aunt Debby say, when she hears we are—engaged?" she asked, half shyly.

"O, she won't say anything. Yes, she will, too; she'll be glad of it, and think I'll settle down—and so I mean to, Evelina."

It was a forlorn sort of engagement. P. stayed for an hour or so, unmolested by the heads of the household, as is too much the fashion, then kissed his Evelina good-bye, and went away with the picture in his pocket, leaving his betrothed to keep her secret to herself, or tell it, and receive the congratulations or the anathemas of the family, as might happen. He meant to go home, tell Aunt Debby, and have a reasonable talk with Miss Gale.

P. was not desperately in love with his Evelina. He had no great amount of affection to bestow on anybody; the fashion of his life had been such as to kill his noblest feelings. Still, he liked the girl; he had been thrown into her society; he was aroused to combat the recreant Snell; spite and fancy together had made him propose the marriage, and now he meant to carry out the plan, thinking it would do as well as anything.

A new feeling of responsibility came upon him; he was ready to settle down to something, to try and fill a man's legitimate position; he would be at the head of a household, and he would be steady now; the wild oats were sown; he'd go home and talk to Miss Gale, and be as reliable as Teddy Green.

Heaven pity this poor fellow! He passed the window of a liquor-store; a store all lighted and brilliant; a window where bottles and decanters, jugs and demijohns and liquor-cases were piled in a great pyramid, the gas-lights showing them off, shining through them, lighting them up; bouquets grouped here and there skilfully, and pictures in the background. The door stood half-open, and two or three of P.'s rowdy friends, in good broadcloth and fine boots, were going in at it.

"Ah, P.! Come in, come in!"

"Give us your arm, old boy; we're in for a particularly jolly time."

"Now we're complete with you here; that's it, my gay boy; here's to the king of the frolic!"

The last speaker took P.'s arm, and pulled him along. One half-uttered "not to-night," one little hesitation on the door-sill, one unfelt pull from the enticing clasp of his arm, and now P. had gone fairly in with them. That talk with Miss Gale; the announcement that was to please our Aunt Debby, were alike forgotten. We are so sorry for you, poor Evelina!

This was early in the evening. P. drank fiery draughts the next hour, and Teddy Green met him on the street with his three tempters, and comrades, giving signs of high excitement. Teddy would not pass him by; he stopped and spoke; took his arm;

invited, urged; secured his company; they walked on together towards home, the shrill songs of the other young men dying in the distance.

"Strange how my head feels!" said P. to Teddy. "It's bursting, Green. I feel the hot blood boiling through it; it sings and roars—can't you hear it?"

Teddy took him home. It was only a little after ten o'clock, and Miss Gale and Aunt Debby were glad to see him in so early. Teddy acted as valet, went with him to his room, bathed his head, bound it up in cold water, got him into bed, gave him a quieting drink, and saw him presently drop asleep. Then he went down to say "good-night, and all safe," to the ladies in the back parlor, and so to go home where all *was* safe, and to a night that was good, with the sleep that blesses honest toil and a clear conscience.

The two ladies did not go early to bed. Their easy manner of life did not tire them greatly; they were used to sit up to all sorts of hours, listening for P.'s uncertain steps. Aunt Debby was nervous, and did not find sleep coming readily, and Miss Gale pitied her, and sat up to read aloud, while the old lady worked quite aimlessly at fancy knitting.

They were sitting thus, rather more peacefully than usual, at twelve o'clock, when there came a rush of feet on the staircase, inarticulate cries that froze the blood with their horrors, and P. tore into the back parlor, his eyes glaring, his frame quivering, and sprung round and round the room as if evading something, crying out, "Laocoön! Laocoön! The great serpent is running after me! Hoy! Ah-a-a! How he tears! he is fast! he is on me!" He stooped as if to wrench away something that had seized his leg. Miss Gale saw that he was insane, and in his frenzied dreams saw the fierce serpents which had wrought horror on the plains of Troy. Marbles, or pictures of that scene, had always had a fascination for P., and now he felt their horror in himself. Again he yelled, "They are both after me! on either side!" and struck out wildly with either arm; then, pale and trembling, crouched behind Miss Gale's chair, clinging to her dress.

We will say for P.'s innocent old aunt that her nephew's agonies of alarm, and the gross impropriety of his taking refuge in her maiden presence, clad only in his night-dress, seemed equally shocking. She gasped out, "Crazy! undressed! What can we do? My dear boy! calm yourself—and put on your pantaloons!"

But P. had more snakes than pantaloons in his mind at that critical moment—the shadow of Miss Gale's chair, and the grasp on her dress, gave him a fancied security. He lifted up her arm, and thrust his eyes and nose under her elbow, so that he could glare at the great crested snakes, mottled with blood, lying now in the far corner.

"Ring the bell, Miss Dean; go for the servants; I can't move!" implored Miss Gale. "Be quick, before he breaks out again!"

"If you fling that footstool true, you might kill it," hissed P. "Its head lies right on the big rose, under the gaslight. Throw it! throw it! before it comes after me again!"

"I see it," said Miss Gale. "It dare not move. I am not afraid of it. Do you know I can charm snakes? Be still, P.;" and she crushed her elbow closer over his eyes, and began soothingly to pat the nervous hands that held her dress. The man-servant and the cook now came, in answer to Aunt Debby's frantic calls. The old lady gasped out, "Mr. Dean is taken crazy, *and he is undressed!*"—one calamity was as great as the other.

The distracted P. was pleased to see, in the black man-servant, the devil come to carry him away; and, in the three hundred pounds avoirdupois of the cook, an embodied nightmare. He ceased to fear the coiled serpents with heads on the rose under the gaslight; gave a howl of terror at the new apparitions, and would have sprung away, and made his capture difficult, had not Miss Gale slipped her arm back upon his neck, and drawn forward the hand she was patting, so, not being a woman all nerves and no muscle, held him fast for a moment, until the servants could seize him.

Aunt Debby devoted herself to draping her nephew's bare knees in a table-cover, while Miss Gale, at his head, put her hand over his eyes, and with firm, quick words of assurance and protection, quieted his fears of snakes and demons, big and little.

The next three days were times of fearful torture to all the Dean household. The ravings of the maniac, the despair of his aunt, the sympathy, and severe duty of nursing, wore on every one. Twice P. had nearly succeeded in killing himself; and one attack on Miss Gale would have resulted in her death, had it not been for her presence of mind.

A week from the day on which he was seized with his delirium, P. had come to himself. He lay exhausted and emaciated on his bed, but was able to remember, to wish, to repent. Miss Gale sat beside him; Aunt Debby lay asleep on the lounge.

"P.," said Miss Gale, "this sickness has worn on you fearfully."

"Yes; and on the poor old lady, too," said P.,

looking over at his aunt, who, in the sickly light of a green damask curtain, looked ghastly as a corpse exhumed days after burial.

"When, and how, will all this come to an end, P.?"

"I don't know—there's so much temptation. If you were to shut me up in a room, and feed me through a hole in the door, I suppose I'd stay there—if the door was locked—and not get drunk."

Miss Gale caught at a new idea. She asked eagerly, "P., would you go to an inebriate asylum?"

"Yes; I'd as soon go there as do anything else. I suppose you want to try everything in my behalf, and you see that legal measures have failed. It is rough work, trying to undo what years of folly and temptation did. When do you want me to go?"

"Day after to-morrow," said Miss Gale, breathlessly, amazed at the sudden acceptance of a scheme which had been only half formed in her own mind. It took shape on the instant, as many vague projects do, when the idea is put into words.

"You must go with me; and you must settle up my business. You might as well begin now. Pull open that drawer, and you'll find any amount of bills, and items, and bank-books, and everything. I *cannot* look after things."

Miss Gale pulled open the drawer, and the heterogeneous mass of letters, bills, receipts, advertisements, play-bills, tickets, and *billets-doux*, gave a severe shock to her orderly soul.

"Can you make head or tail out of them? I can't," said P.

"I *will*," replied Miss Gale. "Perhaps it will interest you if I begin now."

For want of better office arrangements, she took two toilette cushions, and set a knitting-needle up in each. "The bills shall go on one, the receipts on another," she explained. Next, she laid a box by P.'s hand. "That is for letters which you want to keep."

Then a waste-basket was set before the bed. "This is for what is to be thrown away. I will tell you what each is as I open it; if I am throwing away what you want, speak."

The work progressed rapidly.

"How nice it is," said P., "to be able to do things properly! It is a year since I knew how to do anything with that drawer, more than to stuff something more into it; and lately it got so full that I could not open it without something falling out."

"I'm sorry to see so many unpaid bills from tradespeople."

"Yes; they are trifles which it is too much trouble to settle."

"And yet it was not too much trouble to make them. These people may need their money, and your neglect is cruelty. Here is a note from Evelina Snell."

P. held out his hand for it. They had both forgotten Aunt Debby, who lay annihilated, with the exception of her ghastly, worn face, under a down quilt.

"Miss Gale, I want to tell you something," said P. Miss Gale leaned back in her chair, and was all attention. "The other evening I went up to Snell's, and, some way, I got engaged to Evelina. I like her; but I'd never thought of marrying anybody as I know of—but there it is, you see. We're engaged, and I mean to stick to it, if she does. I told her I'd be up next day, and bring her a ring; and here it is a week, and she has not heard a word from me; and if she told her folks maybe they'll twit her about it—I do hate those Snells!—anyway, she'll feel badly, for I think she cares for me, poor girl!"

"And you want me to go and see her, and tell her?"

"Just tell her the truth, where I'm going, and how I've been. Tell her I won't hold her to the promise after that, unless she likes, you know; but you buy a ring and take it; and if she chooses let her have it, so she'll see all is fair on my part. Oh, Miss Gale, I did truly mean to do better! When I found I was engaged, and knew the next thing would be to get married, I *did* mean to act like a man. I was coming home to tell you, and to ask you what I had better do; for I ought to be able to take care of the poor girl, and make her happy; and I wanted to show the Snells I knew what was what, confound them! Then I met three fellows, who pulled me in the saloon with them; they called for what they liked, and you see what has come of it."

Aunt Debby had drawn her face under the down quilt. She had woke up, and innocently shared her nephew's confidences, and was now crying over his miserable, unsatisfactory love affair.

Miss Gale finished the papers; ascertained the amount of debts to be paid, and P. gave her a check for the sum, an amount that was appalling to Miss Gale. The next day, while Aunt Debby was packing P.'s trunk for his departure, Miss Gale set forth on her errand to Evelina. She armed herself with an humble note from P., and a diamond ring. Evelina was looking sad: she had heard of P.'s illness, but not of its nature, and she felt it was cruel that he had sent her no word. Miss Gale thought her a soft, shallow damsel, yet pitied her sincerely.

The ungarnished history narrated by Miss Gale, as a preface to P.'s note and ring, put matters before Evelina in a new light; her common-place and chilly courtship took the golden halo of romance; she could sacrifice herself for P.; she could be like a maiden in a story, and refuse to take back her troth from her self-sacrificing lover. She put on the ring with some spirit. "I shall never desert P.," she said. "The world may turn against him, and be hard on him; all his friends may forsake him, but I will not; we may be poor and despised, but I will not be false."

"That is very kind," said Miss Gale; "but I hope P. will now reform, and not put your love to any such severe test. There will not be any very desperate poverty, for Miss Dean will tie what she has up to his family. The matter for you to look to is that you would be very miserable with a drunken husband; and it would be very hard on all of us to have P. die from the effects of drinking. You must help him to reform. If I were you, I would go and see him, or write to him, and offer to sign the pledge, and urge him to do it also."

"Go see him! O, that would be so queer!" cried Evelina. "Pa would never let me do it; and who ever heard of a *lady* taking the pledge? I should be laughed at every day."

There was no striking anything new out of Evelina. So Miss Gale went home to tell P. that he might still consider himself engaged, and that he must now make himself fit to be the head of a household.

Perhaps it was the exhaustion of illness that made P. so passive in Miss Gale's hands; or, perhaps he really did long to be free of his besetting sin, and was ready to try any means of reformation.

Out of the bustle and temptation of daily life P. was lost for a time, shut into the safety of his asylum. Will years here kill the root of bitterness out of his heart? Will abstinence, advice, healthful living, arm him against the demon of temptation, so that he shall be unmoved when next he meets it face to face?

"What do you think?" asked Dr. Roxwell of the superintendent.

"Sir," replied the wise man, "I could wish we had not inherited tendencies to combat; I could wish we had a right education to assist us; I could wish for an ardent seconding of all our treatment by the patient himself; most of all, I wish that there were a strong foundation of grace in his soul whereon we might build."

CHAPTER THIRTEENTH.

Reasonable Principles Applied.

CHAPTER THIRTEENTH.

Reasonable Principles applied.

P'S. friends visited him in the Asylum. Dr. Roxwell came; Aunt Debby came; Miss Gale came. Evelina did not come, but she sent letters. Evelina was busy playing the role of disconsolate maiden, and in truth she performed the part very well. She talked of her poor P., and his misfortunes; his enemies; his sorrows. After all, one must commiserate the girl, for she led a hard life in the Snell family, who were not above jibes and taunts, and other shabby conduct. Evelina walked through life with drooping head, and her curls very long and lackadaisical; she sighed, and by a judicious neglect of rouge grew pale. Doubtless she was as unhappy as she had capacity to be.

Among the debts which Miss Gale had to settle was one to Mrs. Bently, which took her for the first time to the "Happy Home Hotel." Mrs. Bently, very red-faced and frowzy, with a grease-spotted and frayed poplin gown, and an abundance of tawdry ribbons, was busy behind her bar, dealing out drinks. She asked her visitor to step into the red-curtained sitting-room until the customers had been supplied.

The little room looked as if it had not been swept and dusted for a month; grimy ornaments, which had in their better days graced the Dean mansion, were scattered here and there; a cinder-choked fire struggled feebly in the open Franklin stove, and before it with slipshod feet on the dirty hearth was Mrs. Jillet, leaning back in a red-cushioned rocking-chair, and sound asleep. The ex-housekeeper's face was purple, bloated, and mottled; her cap pushed up behind had settled its soiled border over her eyes; her dress was unfastened, as if to give room to the huge, unhealthy neck, and Mrs. Jillet's heavy breathing was ominous of apoplexy. Even Miss Gale could remember her as a robust, well-dressed, cleanly, busy woman, proud of her position, and careful to fill it well to outward appearance.

Miss Gale sat on a ragged horsehair-covered sofa, and looking about, wondered how P. could have prevailed upon himself to haunt such a place in company with these odious women. Mrs. Bently came in, and seeing her crony asleep, punched her unceremoniously on the head, inquiring if it was proper to lie there snoring at company.

"If it ain't the governess!" cried Mrs. Jillet, arousing. "Well, ma'am, here is an honor, though I've seen you in my room over at the Deans, before they had such a come down as obliged me to leave 'em. How's Miss Dean? She was always rather moping and weak-spirited; she ought to have taken some brandy, or similar, to prop up her constitution. Mrs. Bently, couldn't you bring in a little hot gin, or a drop of rum-and-water for a visitor?"

"No, no, I don't want it—I will not take it," said Miss Gale.

"I will, then," said Mrs. Jillet, calmly; "I feel to need it."

The small servant boy, a scurrilous-looking little wretch, who, poor child, was working out an indebtedness for the whiskey whereof his mother had drank herself to death, brought the rum and water, and Mrs. Bently made a fair mark on the wall with a burnt match which she picked from the floor; the mark was one of many like it, and Mrs. Jillet remarked to the company generally, "when I first came she kept my score private, *now* she marks it out on the wall, and charges high, too."

"I came from Mr. Dean to pay some money he owes you, and to say that you need no longer keep him a room."

As Miss Gale said this, and proffered the amount of the bill she held in her hand, Mrs. Bently de manded tartly,—

"And what is up with Mr. Dean *now*?"

"Mr. Dean is going to reform; he has entered himself at the Inebriate Asylum, and we expect him to come home well."

"Reform! Well, that needn't cut him off from old friends; we have been like own mothers to him, me and Mrs. Jillet."

"Yes, yes, Mrs. Bently, dear," said Mrs. Jillet, in her thick, apoplectic voice, "many's the time he's set here by the fire sipping hot toddy—or similar—to cheer him up, he coming in late and wet; and many's the time he has laid out on that very sofa where Miss Gale's a setting, raging with a headache, and you and me putting cold water on his head and giving him brandy and soda-water. You and me don't get headaches, Mrs. Bently, dear; you and me are stronger-minded."

Shocked at this picture of her poor boy's life, Miss Gale sprung up from the fatal sofa, saying, angrily, "I don't see how a *woman* can keep such a place as this!"

"And what sort of a place is it?" demanded Mrs. Bently.

"A place to destroy men's souls and bodies with drink."

"I've got a license for doing it—my trade's lawful," said Mrs. Bently, coolly.

"A license! a license to commit sin! God does not recognise a right in sin to exist, by giving sin a license."

"*Men* do, and that suits me all the same. I deal with men, not with God," said the blasphemous wretch.

"God will deal with you; mark my words."

"There's your bill, receipted," said Mrs. Bently, having with much reluctance and equal difficulty made an illegible scrawl which was supposed to be her name. "You say Mr. Dean ain't a-coming back; mark *my* words, he *is* coming back."

"Never—I'll keep him away, however low he falls!" said Miss Gale, in great excitement. While Mrs. Bently replied, in equal excitement, "I'll have him back here, if I have him when he's dead!"

Mrs. Jillet had consumed her rum-and-water, and was again nodding in her chair. She roused up again when Miss Gale had departed, and Mrs. Bently sat down near the smouldering fire to talk over the "*impedence*" of the governess. "She thinks she can do for young P. what she did for Mrs. Green, but I'll let her know she can't; I'll have a hand in that matter. How long before he'll come home, think?"

Mrs. Jillet pulled her cap straight; sat up in her chair; drew her shoes on at the heel, and vainly essayed to button the neck of her faded chintz gown. She looked ruefully at her fat, grimy hands, and picked at the folds of her limp skirt. She was moved to these alterations and regrets as to her toilette because the thought of P. had recalled the days of her grandeur, when she ruled the millionaire's household; when the servants feared her; when money was plenty; when her dress was fine; when her room was comfortable, and she fed on the fat of the land; when she was feathering and not destroying her nest. She spoke sententiously:—"See how that house is going down. It was built up on whiskey, and by whiskey it shall fall. Ah! Mrs. Bently, there were days when the cellar was full of the choicest—there were times when one could have white wine or red, without paying for it—there were days when money was plenty, when me and the Deans rolled in gold. I've seen Mr. Dean, P.'s father, as shot hisself, poor soul, get that drunk he could not stir, and at his own table, too, and me going before with a wax-candle in my hand to turn his bed open, while the men brought him up in their arms! For that matter, I've seen his wife—

a handsome creature—so drunk she could not leave ner room. He got tipsy down-stairs, she up-stairs, that was all the difference with them. Well, what now? They're dead. Here's the son—I don't believe he's got forty thousand dollars left out of that million. There's Miss Debby Dean, wilted away like an old faded flower in a bouquet, and no one nigh her but that shabby governess, and only three servants in her house! Well, it was whiskey did that—such money runs as fast it comes. Bless me, to think of it, Mrs. Bently! death, and ruin, and poverty, and destruction to them as is weak enough to be overcome by it! Strange that people can't stand up agin a bit of hot toddy—or similar. Call that brat of a boy to make me a mug of flip, and make it strong."

Mrs. Bently called for the refection for her garrulous crony, and, as soon as it was in her hand, deliberately set another match-mark on the wall.

"You're mighty particular setting down the score," said Mrs. Jillet, tartly. And her hostess responded:—

"I have to be; I've my living to make, and you drink like a fish."

"I know one thing," said Mrs. Jillet: "I've a deal less money than I had when I came to live along with you. And I know another thing: my money gets taken out of my trunk."

"If that's the boy's work, I'll thrash him for it. Drink your flip, and don't worrit. You: money 'll hold out as long as you do."

This was truly a "Happy Home," with the two women quarrelling and cheating, criminating and recriminating each other; the forlorn pot-boy knocked and banged about, overworked, half fed, kept in the whiskey business until, thank God, he was thoroughly sick of it! the miserable topers, coming in to spend the last penny; the sailors and boatmen from the neighboring docks, beguiled to spend their hard-won earnings in deadly poison; the dirt; the riot; the night turned to a sickly, brawling day; the day a grim, straggling fetid twilight;—and the city authorities licensed the horrible den!

"Have they any right to license such places and such traffic?" asked Miss Gale.

"No," said Doctor Roxwell. "To license sin, recognises in sin a right of existence. It has no such right. Sin is an interloper, a rebel, a banned alien; and we are false to God, and to His great government, which beyond dispute sits high over the universe, and over the processes of every inferior court, when we in any way abet or suffer what is evil. To license evil, is to commit the foulest and most shameless evil of all. It is to sin and make others sin with you. For all these things God will bring us into judgment."

We wonder if Aunt Debby had prayed David's prayer, "O, spare me, that I may recover strength, before I go hence and be no more!" After all the weary watching and anxiety of the past years—anxieties which indeed had had no ceasing since her brother the suicide had begun his course of dissipation,—Aunt Debby felt at last that her care was for the present removed: P. was where he would be well taken care of, and she could fold her hands in peace, at least for a season.

Aunt Debby's charity had not been able to expand into an institution for genteel people of fallen fortunes; but now Miss Gale, knowing the healing power of benevolence, was able to lead out Miss Dean's sympathies in good deeds to the suffering; and it was pleasant to see the old lady at her work-table, making up caps or flannels for some unfortunate a few years her senior, or of calico and muslin preparing a wardrobe for some poor babe which, except for her care, might find nothing in a world into which it brought nothing.

Mrs. Green was often made the almoner of these charities; and Aunt Debby could never cease wondering at the changes which she had known in that woman's appearance and history. She would remark to Miss Gale, "A fresh young woman, my dear, whom I was not afraid to let act as a mother to my boy, the last of the Deans; a virtuous, well-mannered person. Then, such a vile outcast that I was afraid to look at her or go near her—a filthy, stupid wretch, maudlin and ragged and a prisoner. Ah! that was what intemperance did for her. Now, a tidy mother of a family, quite respectable and civil; a person I am not afraid to see in my house. That is what temperance has done for her."

As for Teddy, Aunt Debby was pleased to forget what she considered the vast social difference between them, and was ready to make him welcome when he came to call and see if he could render the family any little service in P.'s absence. Besides her benevolence Aunt Debby had her rancors; and the chief portion of her wrath was expended on Mrs. Jillet and Mrs. Bently, whom she considered the chief instruments of her nephew's misfortunes.

Meanwhile, at the asylum, P. was trying that nine pounds of cure which is less valuable than an ounce of prevention.

"How is he getting on?" Dr. Roxwell asked of the superintendent.

"He is one of our most hopeless cases," replied

that responsible person, despairingly. "Not that he drinks—for he has no chance—but there seems absolutely nothing to build a cure on; no self-restraint, no knowledge, no principles. Some one has been terribly to blame about that young man. He would have had a generous heart, if he had had a particle of opportunity. He has a fine physical organization, and naturally a good mind. How can I deal with him? I confess, he seems one of the incurables."

"Apply reasonable principles," suggested the doctor, vaguely.

"Reasonable principles are a mere rope of sand to him."

Dr. Roxwell walked off to where P. lay stretched on a bench in an arbor, looking up into the green vines that swung over his head.

"I hope you're enjoying yourself, Dean."

"I never enjoy myself, and never did," said P.

"Well, when you get out all right, then enjoyment may begin—better late than never."

"All right! Doctor, can you expect a fellow like me to be all right—which means sober—in a city which has more grog-shops in proportion to its inhabitants than any other town or city in the world?"

"That's a very bad notoriety. All of us, as citizens, ought to be ashamed of it, and do our best to bring about a better state of things."

"You'll never bring it about in my day," said P. "It is a good thing, doctor, that you never married, so that you have no sons to be sacrificed. I wonder if you know, if the good parents, the excellent Christians of that city know what is going on about them. Boys of fifteen and sixteen swarming into billiard-saloons, and tippling at liquor-stores. There's no harm in the skilful game of billiards, and nothing illegal in the whiskey traffic; but they're sending us fellows to perdition by the score."

"I thought you didn't believe in a hell, P.!" said the doctor.

"One must believe in what he feels begun within him. I have had delirium tremens, doctor, and then I understood what I used to doubt. While you good people lie in bed asleep, we young chaps drift here and there, now a dance-house, and now a gambling-house open to us—six thousand places where liquor is sold, enticing us on every hand—we are lost before you know it, before we realize it ourselves, there are so many chances of destruction on every side. Aunt Debby used to get me to read on Sundays about a queer old chap called Christian, who had a hump of some kind on his back, and was on a journey. I never got through with it; but one scene used to haunt me, it seemed so like the streets of that famous city of ours, at night. He got into a Valley of the Shadow of Death. I learned the description once, and spouted it at school for an oration. I always had a liking for the horrible; and old Easy blew me up about it, and said such exciting things were unfit for me. I wrote it once on the leaves of my pocket-book. Here the thing is:—

"'We saw there also the hobgoblins, satyrs, and dragons of the pit: we heard also in that valley a continual howling and yelling, as of a people under unutterable misery, who there sat bound in affliction and iron; and over that valley hung the discouraging clouds of confusion; Death also does always spread his wings over it. In a word, it is every whit dreadful, being utterly without order. There was on the right hand a very deep ditch: that ditch is it into which the blind have led the blind in all ages, and have both miserably perished.' (That is the whiskey-seller and the whiskey-drinker, doctor). 'Again, behold! on the left hand there was a very dangerous quag, into which, if even a good man falls, he finds no bottom for his foot to stand on.'

"That's it; that's just the way we fellows are beset, sir—a ditch on one hand, a quag on the other, the devil close behind, and death brooding over all! and—nobody seems to care!"

"'Thus he went on, and I heard him sigh bitterly,'" quoted the doctor. "Very many do care, and are striving to remove temptation, to strengthen you against it also; but it takes a long while for a good cause to gain the mastery, and there have been many hindrances. That burdened Pilgrim, who travelled through the valley you speak of, my dear fellow, had a weapon called *All-Prayer;* and, when he 'walked in the strength of his God,' he walked safely, and the fiends plagued him no more."

"I don't know anything about that," said P. "If ever there was any religious instinct in me, it has been all burned out by whiskey-drinking."

"See here!" said the doctor; "you are in the dumps to-day. You are the victim of physical depression, occasioned by the lack of an accustomed stimulant; and the depression of the body reacts on the mind. Let us talk of something more cheerful. You are engaged to be married, my boy."

"Yes," said P., indifferently.

"Then you must rouse up, and do great things for the girl you love."

"Evelina is not the sort of girl one is roused to do great things for, doctor. If a girl had a high purpose, an earnest way of living and speaking, like Miss Gale for instance, it seems as if she might inspire even a fellow like me to try and be worthy of her. I don't find fault with Evelina. She's as good as the rest of the girls I've known, and quite good enough for me. None of these girls I've seen can be like those of old times, for whose sake the knights errant did such grand deeds."

"There are grander deeds done now a days, and grander women who inspire them," said the doctor, smiling.

"I wish I could have seen some of them," said P. "But of course, doctor, I mean to marry Evelina, for I said I would. I don't look forward to any very charming times. I will be drinking, and seeing snakes maybe; and Evelina will be doing her hair in curl-papers, and crying."

"If you have made up your mind to that life, I don't see what use it is for you to be here, Dean."

"No more do I; and when the thirst is strong in me some day, I'll break jail and away."

"See here, my boy; is not the saving of your soul worth striving for? Can you not see your duty to yourself and to the world, and stand up to it like a man? When you know that only one evil habit stands between you and all reasonable enjoyments, can you not resolve to be free of that habit? Can you deliberately dare all the horrors of disease and insanity which drinking will bring upon you?

"Doctor, my parents gave me love of drink for an inheritance; my nurses poisoned me; my aunt and my teachers extravagantly indulged me; society tempted me in every form; the law licensed my enemies to destroy me. Men and women; parents and acquaintances; civil law and the avarice of strangers, have leagued with the devil against me; and do you expect me to withstand all this? I'm a doomed man."

"No man can be doomed against his will," said the doctor.

"Will! My will is demoralized," said P., languidly.

CHAPTER FOURTEENTH.

Society renders a Verdict.

"Gold, still gold; it haunted *him* yet.
At the Golden Lion the inquest met;
Its foreman a carver and gilder."

CHAPTER FOURTEENTH.

Society renders a Verdict.

ONE year passed while our young man was in the asylum. Nothing but the most earnest endeavors of his friends, the persuasion of their constant visits, and the frantic representations of Aunt Debby, would have detained there so long a patient, who, from his first entrance, had been considered nearly hopeless. P. had long ago given up all thought or wish of reformation, and only desired to return to his old companions, and the riotous indulgence of his city life. Whenever he hinted or plainly expressed such wish, visits, letters, entreaties, compelled him to remain at his retreat. To get home without this preliminary excitement, he made his escape from the asylum on the twenty-fifth of January, 1869, and on the following day presented himself at his own house, to the distress of his aunt, while Miss Gale was not at all surprised, having been for some time convinced that it was thus that he would return.

These two women made the most pitiful efforts to welcome their wanderer, to conceal their fears, to show confidence in him; and, while they pretended to trust, sought really to watch and to control. We doubt not that P. saw through the poor pretences of his aged aunt, and they should have put him to shame; but shame was dead.

The affection of Evelina Snell could not have been expected to survive a year of absence. Of late her letters had been few and short; but the Snells were a large family of daughters, and lovers had not been so plentiful that Evelina had been tempted actually to transfer her allegiance; so P. still considered himself an engaged man. The parental Snell took occasion to ask P. what were his intentions, and how soon he proposed to marry. P. politely replied that he should be only too happy, whenever it suited his Evelina.

"I must take opportunity to inquire into your affairs," said Mr. Snell, pompously. His bloated purple face, and arrogant voice, vexed P., who saw in him a former tempter, and, we might say, robber; and he tartly made answer that he had very small affairs to look into; his guardians and executors, and the public generally, had stolen from him to such an extent that he had no property left worth inquiring after.

"How can you expect to marry my daughter?" demanded the irate Snell.

"That is for her to say," replied P. "I have you, for one, to thank for what I am."

Father Snell informed his family that he was convinced that "P. had gone to the dogs, was unworthy the Snell countenance, and that Evelina could doubtless make a much better match." Three days before, Evelina would have scouted this idea; but she had lately danced with a man with a mustache, who said he was an Italian count; and but a few hours before her father declared P.'s canine whereabouts, Evelina had received a bouquet and a poetical note from the "count;" she therefore simply sulked at her parent's remarks, and held her decision in abeyance.

Restraint had been succeeded by excess. Solomon perceived that the washed sow straightway bolted off to the mire, there to wallow with increased satisfaction; and so P., after the enforced abstinence of his asylum, returned with avidity to "brandy, whiskey, gin—an' similar," as Mrs. Jillet informed Mrs. Bently with much secret pleasure.

"Yes," said Mrs. Bently, with a smack of triumph in her voice. "That upstart of a governess thought she could keep him all his life in leading-strings, and even packed him off to an inebriate asylum! I wonder does she want to marry him, or want his money?"

"Pooh! no, Mrs. Bently, dear. She's old enough to be his mother; and as to the money, that's gone to the winds: he's used up about all he has, I'm thinking! He's like me!" cried Mrs. Jillet, finishing her toddy, and getting angry, as often happened, at "Mrs. Bently, dear." "Like me! My score's longer than my purse has got to be. I had a nice mint of money for a lone woman when I came here, but it's gone fast, and I ain't spent it. I'm robbed—*robbed*—ROBBED, I tell you, and I'll set the police after you, Mrs. Bently, that I will. You vile hussy, to rob an old friend, and she in poor health, and all alone in the world!" And Mrs. Jillet fell a sobbing into the folds of her dirty apron, while Mrs. Bently, with words wonderfully like swearing, went out and gave short measure to her customers, and slapped her forlorn Ganymede, dismal bearer of pewter cups to these infernal gods.

Into such a reeking Gehenna, our P., the child of luxury, spoiled Heir of a Million, staggered often; to lie on the foul bed, or the ragged haircloth-covered sofa, stupidly drunk, or maybe racked with pain, or seeing in these greasy red-faced harridans the demons of his delirious agonies.

Nor here alone did delirium come upon him. At his own house he sprang screaming from the table, and seized the carving-knife to put an end to himself. Miss Gale wrenched the weapon from him, and he then flashed up-stairs, going on all-fours, and howling like a hyena; after him went Miss Gale, at a frantic pace; by her side ran the black man-servant, with his eyes starting from his head, and sweat rolling down his face; the fat cook, with a toasting-fork, whereof the prongs were ornamented with half-cooked cheese, lumbered breathlessly to the rescue; the housemaid stumbled on in haste, making ineffectual efforts to hold up her dress from under her feet, and Aunt Debby, white and trembling, weeping and moaning, feebly brought up the rear of this domestic rout.

Such a scene was succeeded by days of watching by P.'s sick-bed, when his life was despaired of, and those who loved him best having become hopeless of his repentance, even wished that he might die without further sin or pain.

Miss Gale had been a most devoted friend of her former pupil. She had watched his wayward track these several years, toiling for his welfare like a sister; but now, if it had not been for Aunt Debby, she would have returned to her own friends, and left him to "gang his lane."

Meanwhile P. had neglected Evelina, and the "Count" with the moustache had been attentive, he rolled up his eyes, and talked of the "golden-haired beauty of the North;" he had sighed in a manner that Evelina considered most romantic. She assured her most intimate friend that if she broke her engagement with P., P. would kill himself; if she was true to P. the "Count" would be heartbroken.

At such a juncture of affairs, P. by no means bettered his prospects by appearing before Evelina in a state of intoxication; he came for an evening call, and though not ungraceful naturally, he stepped through the trailing folds of her rose-colored muslin at his very entrance, and while Evelina, burning with wrath and mortification, seated herself on a sofa and strove to conceal the rent, he placed himself at her side, and fell heavily against her shoulder, remarking, "You look deuced pretty to-day, Evelina—wish I'd brought you a present."

"I wish you'd behave!" cried the poor girl, passionately. "You are drunk, you know you are, and how dare you come here and act so? I never want to see you again."

"That's a good one, when we're engaged!" jeered P.

"I'll not be engaged to you another day!" cried Evelina, much excited, snatching off the ring Miss Gale had brought her, and thrusting it at him. "You are a cruel, wicked wretch, and if you cared one bit for me, you'd have done better long ago."

P. was too little master of his own thoughts or acts than to understand what he did, or his Evelina said. He had no consciousness of how he left the house, or how or when he got home—but he found himself lying in his own bed towards noon next day, and was conscious that he had quarrelled with Miss Snell. His coat and vest were hanging from the seat of a chair, his pocket-book, knife, and a ring that looked strangely like the one Evelina had worn, lay on the floor as they had slipped from his pocket.

"I wonder if I'm out of that noose?" said P. to himself, regarding the ring. Then better thoughts came to him. "I wonder if I behaved badly, and if I've made the poor girl feel unhappy? Confound it all, I hope not! What luck I have! just a curse to myself and everybody. Would it have been better to marry and settle down? *could* I have settled down, and been sober, and gone into business, if I *had* married? maybe not. The world is very hard on me!"

He dressed and rung for some breakfast to be sent up to him. When the man brought in the tray, two notes lay beside the coffee cup. When alone, he opened them—one was from Evelina, formally breaking off their engagement, on account of his ill conduct. Had this been alone, P. might have been penitent, and though he would not have sought to renew the broken bonds, he would have begged pardon for past offences; but the excellent father of Evelina must needs send P. a proud, taunting epistle, forbidding him the house, reflecting on his ruined fortunes and dishonored name, and stating that he had other and better prospects for his daughter than marriage with a penniless drunkard.

From another man, P. might have borne this as deserved; but not from Snell, who had made him drunk at his table, himself an habitual tippler, and who had lived like a parasite on P. in his more palmy days, draining him of a part of his million.

P. was in a paroxysm of fury; he was in a state of mind where he could have killed Snell; but not seeing him, his rage rebounded upon himself, and he rushed off to a saloon where bad whiskey and bad company alike abounded. Here, through the warm summer afternoon, he drank and played cards, in the fashion of many, who, angry at being condemned as unworthy, proceed at once to show the condemnation just.

Twelve, one, two; the night was wearing away, and still Aunt Debby waited for her boy to come. She feared evil for him, for already Miss Gale had surmised that the engagement with Evelina was broken. Miss Gale had gone to P.'s room soon after his departure, and had found on the table a little heap of fragments of written note-paper, and beside them the well-known ring which she had taken to Evelina. She told Miss Debby of this in the evening, and when the gentle old aunt began to lament that every one was unjust and unkind, and to throw a halo of romance over her nephew's lawless life, by crying out that his affections were trifled with, and that his heart was broken, Miss Gale did not contradict the assertion, for she knew it is easier to believe our dear ones sinned against than sinning.

"We must go out of town for the hot weather; and now that Miss Snell has treated him badly, our boy will be willing to go with us—indeed, I could not go and leave him; and we will take him to the mountains and make him happy. After all," added Aunt Debby, piously, "this affliction may be a means of good to him, and sorrow may reform him."

Then, as it was very late, the two went to their

rooms, and perhaps Miss Gale fell asleep; but Aunt Debby left the gas burning and sat up in bed in night-gown and cap, reading her Bible and waiting for P. She may have had some revelation of the possibilities and opportunities which she had neglected—some vision of shining heights where she might have walked even in this present life, as she read and waited, for the leaves of the Book were very wet with her last tears.

Three o'clock. The alabaster clock in the back parlor, the rosewood clock in the dining-room, the mahogany clock in the hall, the bronze clock in Aunt Debby's room, and the gilt clock in P.'s room, chimed out the hour, one after the other. P.'s clock lagged, like its master; and now, as the key turned in the latch, and P. came in, Aunt Debby rose from her bed, and put her head out from her door:—

"I'm glad you are in safe, my dear boy!"

"Plague on it! why *will* you always wait up for a fellow! Of course I'll get in safe; and if I don't, it would be no matter."

Thus spoke the young man on whom the Snell family had passed their verdict—a verdict in which we must now acquiesce.

Yet a little later, and Aunt Debby knocked at her nephew's door, and then went in.

A dim, gray twilight filled the room, and P. was in bed.

"I could not go to sleep when your last word was cross, my poor dear boy," said the old lady, tremulously. "I must give you a chance to speak like yourself." She sat down by his bed, and smoothed his hot forehead with her wrinkled, soft hand. "My heart aches for you, my dear child; I know you are unhappy. Has Evelina——"

"I'm done with her, and glad of it," growled P.

"My dear! Remember, P., that there is always one who loves you better than life, and will always love and pray for you. Oh, my child, I'm afraid I have done very wrong by you, though I meant well, and sinned only through ignorance. And yet we may be to blame for our ignorance. If my folly has brought you to these sins and sorrows, Oh, my boy, forgive me! forgive me!"

"There! there! Aunt Debby. You have always done well enough—better than I deserve; what wrong there is, is my part. Go to bed, Aunt Debby; you'll get cold and tired out."

Five o'clock. All the clocks in the house had told the time to all the others. Miss Gale is running into P.'s room without the ceremony of a knock—"P., wake up! wake up!"

Now she shakes him by the shoulder, and cannot break the deep sleep of intoxication. "Wake up! Oh, wake up! Aunt Debby is dying! Come! She asks for you!" This shouted in the sleeper's ear; but he only turned heavily on his pillow with a muttered curse, swung his arm into the air and let it fall—he could not be aroused.

The man-servant had gone for the doctor and a friend; the cook, in a wide-bordered cap, stood, sleepily amazed, at the bed's foot; the housemaid, dropped in a little heap on the floor, cried some sincere tears, for she really loved Aunt Debby. Miss Gale stood by the pillows which bolstered up her friend, and wiped her damp face, fanning her gently to assist the laboring breath. For a moment or two Miss Dean seemed to desire her nephew's presence, and looked wistfully about for him. Then she mercifully lost the knowledge of his absence. She leaned back more restfully, and drew a deep breath or two. Then the constant love and compassion she had shown to her nephew she whispered faintly—"Good-night, and God bless you, my dear boy!" her head dropped forward, the doctor came in, and the servants opened the shutters to the red light of morning. Aunt Debby had gone where the afflicted are comforted, the feeble are strengthened, and "God shall wipe away all tears from their eyes!"

P. rang his bell twice next morning between ten and eleven. After a little delay, the housemaid answered it, red-eyed and hesitating.

"Where's that man, that I must keep ringing in this way, and he does not come?" growled P., sick and cross.

"If you please, sir, he has gone to the undertaker's with a message. Your aunt died early this morning, Mr. Dean."

"And why was I not called?" demanded P., lifting his head.

"Miss Gale couldn't waken you, sir; she came when your aunt asked for you, but you were too heavy asleep."

"There; go down stairs, and let me alone."

Presently Miss Gale came to the room. "P., the last words she said were to you, 'God bless you!' Oh, P., think of that blessing, and try and get it!"

P. sobbed, "I'm not worthy of a blessing! Poor dear old Aunt Debby, she's gone! her troubles are ended! I wish mine were!"

"They would be ended by seeking God, my friend,—in no other way. To those who have not sought Him, the end of life is but the beginning of sorrows."

Aunt Debby was buried. P. stayed quietly in the house, with Miss Gale, until after the funeral. In the evening after they returned from the cemetery, Dr. Roxwell and Aunt Debby's lawyer came with the good woman's will. Now that she was gone, the house, and all that it contained, came, by the terms of his grandfather's will, into P.'s hands unconditionally; so long as Miss Dean had lived nothing could be sold, and she had her right there. Aunt Debby's own little fortune had been reduced several times by paying P.'s debts; she left him the remainder in such shape that he could have only the income unless he entirely reformed, and in that case he could have the capital to invest in business.

"My money is all gone," said P., gruffly. "I don't see why she could not give me hers out and out."

"Because," said Dr. Roxwell, severely, "she knew that it would be all gone, too, in a short time, and she has arranged for you to have a little income to save you from absolute poverty."

The following morning, at breakfast, P. asked Miss Gale what they were to do now.

"I shall go to my uncle," said Miss Gale. "And if you will go too, and reform, you will find plenty to help you, and happiness in store for you."

"I don't intend to reform; I've tried a dozen times and have failed. There is nothing to run this establishment on now, at least *I* can't make the income do it, and I am not domestic. I shall sell out. Aunt Debby left you a number of mementoes, and I shall add some more which I don't like to see sold. I wish you'd send them off to your uncle's, pay and dismiss the servants, and get things in order for me—you have always been so kind."

After that, P. was seldom sober enough to look after anything: some nights he came home, others he came not. Miss Gale rendered her verdict to Dr. Roxwell: "The poor boy is an utterly abandoned and hopeless fellow. I never saw such greedy running after sin."

Miss Gale bade her old pupil good-bye with an aching heart. He was too drunk to understand what she said to him. Next day, the red flag was flying from doors and windows of the Dean mansion; and house and furniture, family plate and family pictures, books and mementoes, long ago Christmas and birthday gifts, went under the auctioneer's hammer.

The sum obtained by this sale was put in P.'s hands, and he began a reckless course of extravagance that surpassed all his former proceedings. He hired two men-servants, bought a carriage and pair of horses, went to a fashionable hotel, and for three months was the scandal of his native city. "Society," that potent, variable, Proteus-shaped divinity, pronounced an irrevocable judgment on young P. Dean. P. was called to the bar of Society, and declared a debased, ungentlemanly vagabond, unfit for genteel notice.

P. was ostracised by Society, by Pincham, Snell, and even by Binkle, and scores of other good people; but, driven from this reputable and accomplished circle, Mrs. Bently and Mrs. Jillet would yet receive him with open arms.

CHAPTER FIFTEENTH.

And so does the Coroner.

"And the jury debated from twelve to three
What the verdict ought to be,
And they brought it in as a *felo de se*."

CHAPTER FIFTEENTH.

And so does the Coroner.

GAMBLING and drinking made short work with the funds P. had obtained by the sale of his house and furniture. There came a day when coachman and valet left P. because their wages were not paid. The carriage and horses were sold on account of the bill for keep at the livery-stable; the coachman, by a well-timed suit, getting part of the price for the money due him, the other servant having paid himself by a watch, a ring, and a dressing-case. Some little time after this P. left the fashionable hotel, absolutely ejected, because of his inability to settle for his board; and his trunks being detained for debt, this heir of a great fortune, who had lived in luxury, went down to Mrs. Bently's "Happy Home Hotel," on Water street, with only a portmanteau of clothing, a few dollars in his pocket, and no trinket of value left him except the emerald ring on his finger.

The Happy Home was the chosen resort of vermin innumerable and unmentionable; grimy windows shut out the view of the foul street, with ragged urchins playing in the oozing slime of the sewers. From the dark kitchen came up a stench of onions, tobacco, gin, and stale mutton; through all the dingy rooms rang the voices of Mrs. Bently and Mrs. Jillet, quarrelling over scores and money, and the short yelps of a starved dog, and the impish little slave, whose mother had died of Mrs. Bently's whiskey.

Mrs. Bently's discerning eye read the history of her dear Mr. Dean's misadventures, and comprehended the low ebb of his fortunes.

"I've been a losing money, Mr. Dean, sir," she said, on the second day of his stay, "and I've made new rules. Just for business sake, would you pay me an advance, sir?"

P. paid her ten dollars.

"I'll not trust him, he's run out," said Mrs. Bently to Mrs. Jillet; "I'll keep paid ahead, and when he's no more money out he goes, and so does some other people as sets theirselves up for big folks."

"Be careful, Master Dean, dear, she's a thief; she's been robbing of me; keep your portmanteau locked up, and look out for your pocket-book, or let me keep it for you," said Mrs. Jillet, in confidence to P.

"There's nothing in it to tempt either of you," said P., with a shrill, bitter laugh.

Who would now recognise P., in clothes frayed and made shabby by rows in low doggeries, and nights spent in station-houses, his patent-leather boots cracked and worn, his hat battered and water-stained, his shirt-bosom soiled and rumpled? Was this the fashionable young gentleman who had made New Year's calls, and gone to the parties of the wealthiest in the city, whom mothers and daughters had courted and petted, and hoped to win?

The few possessions in the portmanteau mysteriously disappeared. Mrs. Jillet and Mrs. Bently may have wanted handkerchiefs and socks. When Mrs. Bently boldly dunned for another advance of board, P. went to the pawnbroker's, to sell the emerald ring. That brought him twenty-five dollars, and Mrs. Bently got fifteen, to stop her mouth for three weeks to come.

Two days after the three weeks were ended, Mrs. Bently, Mrs. Jillet, and P. sat about a little table drinking and playing cards. It would have been hard to tell which was the most fearsome sight—these two hideous old women, or the wrecked and wretched young man who was their victim.

"Bring us some rum and water, some flip—or similar—I'm thirsty," said Mrs. Jillet.

The shocking little boy, an animated scarecrow, brought the refection; all drank, and Mrs. Bently won P.'s money.

"You owe me a quarter."

"Can't pay it—I'm dead broke," said P., surlily.

"Then, where is your board coming from?" demanded Mrs. Bently.

"From nowhere—all's up with me," said P.

"You *shall* pay it. It is two days overdue, you villain. And you've a debt for two dollars at the bar, and not a rag of baggage worth seizing, you thief. To come here trying to cheat a lone woman as always treated you like a mother!" shrieked the drunken landlady.

"You've shared plenty of my money, you vile Jew!" said P., enraged. "I leave it to Mrs. Jillet, if you have not had round hundreds from me, and robbed me most scandalously."

"I'll call the police to you!" yelled Mrs. Bently. "If you can't pay up, you can go. Out with you, or I'll put you out!"

"Maybe he'll have some more money in a day or two," said Mrs. Jillet, longing to oppose Mrs. Bently, whom she both feared and hated.

"Not to-morrow, nor any other day," said P., doggedly.

The wind howled through the streets; the sleet rattled against the windows; it was an evening early in the November of 1870. A storm had raged for two days, and it was bitterly cold. The hour approached midnight; without all was darkness, except for the flaring of the street-lamps; the few forlorn wayfarers who yet wandered in the streets shivered and hid their chill hands in their clothing, while they slipped and stumbled on the icy pavement. The "rum and similar" had been drunk from the dirty glasses on Mrs. Bently's table; the poor old lamp burnt low; the greasy cards lay scattered on the floor. P., sitting there, gaunt, haggard, with a deathly whiteness settled on his pinched face, his thin worn clothes buttoned closely about his wasted frame, and his feet showing through the broken leather of his boots, might have been a sight to move any compassion but Mrs. Bently's. Still she taunted him, and threatened—still forbade him to go to his room until he made her another payment; still roughly bade him go out from her doors, and walk in the streets, like the vagabond he was.

And this woman had held him in her arms as a babe; had lived under his roof; could remember all the splendor of his early surroundings; had herself tempted him, and dragged him down to this dire ruin on this bleak November night.

There was no fire now in the rusty, broken stove. Mrs. Jillet wrapped her miserable shawl about her, and staggered off to her bed. The forlorn servant-boy was forgetting his troubles as he fell asleep on a pile of rags under the counter of the bar, sharing his bed with the hungry cur. Mrs. Bently shook her fist in P.'s face!

"Begone! I tell you. I'll harbor you no longer under my roof, you poverty-struck, lean-faced scamp!"

P. rose, and with unsteady step passed out into the night. Up and down the streets he wandered, walking mechanically to keep from freezing, the liquor dizzying his brain at first, so that he could realize nothing. As the cold air sobered him more and more, the apprehension of his degraded and outcast lot came to him; all hope was dead; life was a burden and a curse; he had sunk now so low that there was no eye to pity and no hand to save; to live was to be cold, sick, starved, weary, and despised. Where should he look for safety? Even then Dr. Roxwell would have welcomed and rescued him, but P. had sedulously kept out of his sight these several months. Miss Gale, with love and pity like a sister's, would have received this prodigal, have fed and clothed him, and helped him to help himself. But to neither of these did the unfortunate turn in the hour of his extremity.

On this very night Evelina had married her bogus "Count" with the mustache, and all the Snell family, thoroughly deceived, had celebrated the wedding, and the house was now strown with fading flowers and relics of the marriage feast; and forgotten gaslights were burning dimly in the gray light of the breaking day. In all the festive gathering, no gay heart had thought of him, once rich and jolly, first at the dance and in the wine-room. He had passed out of all their careless lives and from their fickle hearts, and standing now in the narrow, dismal street, the sleet freezing to his shabby garments and to his shaggy hair, P. realized that he had outlived his fortunes, and debated whether he should now brave the misery of life or the misery of death. He knew well what was the growing pain of living; he cared little what might come for him when life was done. He would give himself no time for thought; he could at least escape cold, scorn, famine, the pain that preyed upon him day after day. Then he turned from the circle of light in which he had stood by the lamp-post, and ran as quickly as his weak, trembling, chilled feet could take him, down by the "Happy Home Hotel," around the corner by the groggery, by the great warehouse, where once cargoes of rum from the West Indies had been landed for his grandfather, along past the forsaken stall where in daylight some imp of darkness dealt out "Tom and Jerry" to sailors; on, on, along the wharf, out on the pier, where the black water slips up and down; one plunge—and he is done with the tempters and temptations and the miseries that have dogged him and preyed upon him here.

Did he wildly repent? Did he struggle to the surface of the icy water, and cry out in his despair, and strike out feebly with unnerved arm, and sink, and rise once more gasping in agony, and go down hopeless?

"Hoy! Hoy! Halloo—a man drowning!"

"Hah! did you see that fellow going by, and then a plunge? Lend a hand, here! Somebody gone in drunk or crazy. Help him out."

Where did they come from, and what were they—these men that suddenly swarmed out on the wharf, gaunt and uncanny in the dim morning twilight? All had seemed deserted just now, and here were some dozen people looking out over the water, getting loose a boat, talking, ordering, conjecturing—all intent on saving him who went down a moment ago. Policemen, stray sailors, a stall-keeper, wharf-rats, a thief looking for junk, a runaway apprentice, hunting for a vessel to carry him far from a plundered master—these are intent on gaining back to life P., born heir to a million, and now a beggared suicide!

They have him at last; water streaming from the bony form; slime making tattered boots and clothes and unkempt hair more wretched and loathsome still; his face set in some grim agony—the last mortal throe, when, perhaps with the water rushing in his ears, and choking his breath, he had realized what future stretched before him, long as eternity!

"I know him," said the policeman, looking curiously into the dead face. "He was an uptown 'swell;' he's name is Dean."

"Belike he ain't dead," said a wharf-rat. "He only went in a bit ago; maybe we can bring him to."

"He belongs up here at Happy Home, kep' by an old hag named Bently," said the stall-keeper. "He's bought several drinks of me."

"Let's carry him there," urged the apprentice, manfully catching hold of the water-dripping boots, while the sailor lifted the shoulders, the wharf-rat ran for a doctor, and the policeman walked alongside. So, early in the morning, while Mrs. Bently was first opening her bar-room to steal the strength and sense of poor day-laborers passing by, a small procession stopped at her door. She trembled first, at sight of the policeman; then, perceiving his errand, took courage, and cried out, "Don't bring *that* in here, to spoil my custom! He don't belong here."

"He do too," said the stall-man, stoutly. "I seen him here."

"Take it out; he's in debt for his board!" screamed Mrs. Bently.

"Don't be a brute," said the policeman, pushing into the sitting-room, and pulling forward the worn sofa. "Bring blankets, and make a fire. Off with his clothes, some of you, and treat him according to the laws for folk found drowned! Here's the doctor."

The doctor looked "no hope," but he went to work at his patient, confiscating some of Mrs. Bently's drinkables, to her great wrath, and Mrs. Jillet's secret delight.

They ceased their efforts after a time. "No use; he was dead before he came out of the water. Notify the coroner; straighten him out. Woman! can't you bring me a couple of sheets, and lay him out decently?"

"He's nothing to me," said Mrs. Bently, defiantly, "and in debt for his board."

Mrs. Jillet, however, found a shirt and a pair of

socks. The doctor had a shutter taken from the back window, laid it over the rickety table where last night P. had played cards and drank his last dram, then the body was laid thereon, and in the afternoon the coroner came with his men, and took possession cf Mrs. Bently's room. He was drowned, no doubt of that. Was it accidental drowning? was it deliberate suicide? was it the result of drunkenness? "Suicide, likely; he looks miserable enough," said one man.

"Drunkenness, probably; nine-tenths of such deaths are the result of that," said another. "Such dens as these are as bad on population as a contagious disease."

Then testimony was taken, what little could be gathered; and, while there was a question in the coroner's mind as to his verdict, Mrs. Jillet urged:—

"Don't make it a suicide, sir! I don't think he did it a purpose. No; he belonged to one of the first families in the city, and he was worth a million of dollars the day he was born. His house was a palace; he threw his money away like dirt, sir; he had everything heart could wish; Snell's daughter was engaged to him; Pincham and Binkle were administrators of his estate; he visited the finest people of town; Mr. Dean he was, sir; and had his own carriage not a year ago. Don't call it suicide!"

"Found drowned." Yes; that was the way it was read by all the city next day. That was the way it reached Teddy Green's ears the night of the inquest, when P.'s body lay still in the "Happy Home," waiting early morning interment by the city authorities.

Teddy went for Dr. Roxwell, that they might carry the dead man to one of their houses—for Teddy was living in very respectable style now—and give it a becoming burial. Teddy then went to Mrs. Bently's in haste, while the doctor was to follow with a hearse, a coffin, and a shroud.

Mrs. Bently was in her bar in an angry, excited frame of mind, declaring that "the corpse had scared off her customers." Mrs. Jillet had gone in to look at the body, for some reason or another, and a loud crash resounded through the house as Teddy's hand was on the door-latch. Mrs. Jillet had been seized with a fit of apoplexy, and had fallen against the unsteady table, throwing it over. A ghastly sight met Teddy's eyes; the corpse thrown on the floor, the table and shutter resting upon it, and Mrs. Jillet prostrate, with purple face and foaming lips.

In a few moments the doctor arrived, to render what aid he could to the once active housekeeper, and the undertaker came with him, to wrap the dead pauper in a costly shroud, and put him to sleep in such a coffin as had held his father and grandfather.

As the hearse was about starting, and the carriage for the doctor and Teddy Green was coming up, Mrs. Bently grasped the doctor's arm. "You must give me a hospital certificate for her, doctor dear, and I'll pack her off early in the morning. She has been living on my bounty this many years, and I ain't going to keep her a day longer."

The doctor wrote the required document on a blank leaf from his note-book, and handed it over. "I'll send a carriage and nurse here after her. You have small charity, Mrs. Bently. I remember when you were glad enough to have her acquaintance, and you have followed her up ever since, until she has become that mass of disease." They were looking at the unhappy Mrs. Jillet, who was stretched on a bed rudely made on the floor, and her heavy breathing resounded through the small room.

While Mrs. Jillet lay thus unconscious, and the doctor followed to his own house the hearse that bore the body of P. Dean, Mrs. Bently was scrupulously searching the remaining effects of her quondam crony, and was rewarded by finding a twenty-dollar note sewed into the lining of her last dress. This, Mrs.

Bently confiscated for some unexplained indebtedness; and thus, when Mrs. Jillet, once the self-satisfied and self-serving housekeeper of the Dean family, went to the city hospital next day, she went penniless and in tatters.

A funeral next day. Four bearers in a carriage; Aunt Debby's old pastor in another carriage; then Miss Gale and her uncle; next the doctor and Teddy. So they went to the cemetery on which wealth and nature had lavished adornment, to the Dean lot with its four graves and four grand monuments, and with a fifth grave yawning open, where the doctor would put another monument, telling that P. Dean had died, aged twenty-six years and six months.

A fearful family burial-place that, where, out of five graves, only one holds a body laid down in good hope of a glorious immortality; a very dreary place, where, out of five dead, you can count a vender of strong drink, and three of its victims; a horrible place, where the suicides father and son, and the mother no less a suicide, sleep side by side! Full many cemeteries are written with these terrible tragedies of intemperance.

The short ceremony is over, and all may go home. The wealthy Dean family is extinct, destroyed by that whereon it rose to splendor. It was built up on woes and curses and ruined souls, and they are all its history!

* * * * * * *

Miss Gale sat at breakfast at the old doctor's table; he was stirring his coffee, and reading the morning paper. He laid it down and looked at Miss Gale, and Miss Gale's uncle. "Here is a story of retribution," he said. "It was rather late in life that I began to consider my religious duties, or look into the ways of Providence; but, in a dozen years I have seen a good many especial providences, and some judgments falling heavily in this life." The doctor was aged, and given to prosing, but his guests were indulgent. He took up his paper and searched for a paragraph, then read aloud:—

"'A miserable groggery on Water street, called the Happy Home Hotel, kept by a Mrs. Bently, was burned at eleven o'clock last evening. A boy, who slept under the counter in the bar-room, escaped. Mrs. Bently being probably too drunk to arouse easily, was burned to death. It was not known that she was in the house until it was too late to rescue her.'" It was savagely added, most likely by the hand of Teddy Green: "If all the other groggeries of this description which the city boasts, and their incorrigible keepers, met a like fate, it would result in an immense saying of the life and property yearly destroyed by them."

"Yes," said the doctor, "that is retribution. First and last, that woman was the ruin of our unfortunate friend."

"There were so many agents in his ruin," said Miss Gale, "that we cannot lay the whole burden upon one of them."

"Poor fellow! poor fellow!" sighed the old gentleman. "He had a hard time in life; he was destroyed by having everything he wanted, and no restraint that he needed; he was born Heir to a Million too Much."

THE END.

STANDARD AND POPULAR BOOKS

PUBLISHED BY

PORTER & COATES, PHILADELPHIA, PA.

WAVERLEY NOVELS. By SIR WALTER SCOTT.

*Waverley.
*Guy Mannering.
The Antiquary.
Rob Roy.
Black Dwarf; and Old Mortality.
The Heart of Mid-Lothian.
The Bride of Lammermoor; and A Legend of Montrose.
*Ivanhoe.
The Monastery.
The Abbott.
Kenilworth.
The Pirate.
The Fortunes of Nigel.
Peveril of the Peak.
Quentin Durward.
St. Ronan's Well.
Redgauntlet.
The Betrothed; and The Talisman.
Woodstock.
The Fair Maid of Perth.
Anne of Geierstein.
Count Robert of Paris; and Castle Dangerous.
Chronicles of the Canongate.

Household Edition. 23 vols. Illustrated. 12mo. Cloth, extra, black and gold, per vol., $1.00; sheep, marbled edges, per vol., $1.50; half calf, gilt, marbled edges, per vol., $3.00. Sold separately in cloth binding only.

Universe Edition. 25 vols. Printed on thin paper, and containing one illustration to the volume. 12mo. Cloth, extra, black and gold, per vol., 75 cts.

World Edition. 12 vols. Thick 12mo. (Sold in sets only.) Cloth, extra, black and gold, $18.00; half imt. Russia, marbled edges, $24.00.

This is the best edition for the library or for general use published. Its convenient size, the extreme legibility of the type, which is larger than is used in any other 12mo edition, either English or American.

TALES OF A GRANDFATHER. By SIR WALTER SCOTT, Bart. 4 vols. Uniform with the Waverley Novels.

Household Edition. Illustrated. 12mo. Cloth, extra, black and gold, per vol., $1.00; sheep, marbled edges, per vol., $1.50; half calf, gilt, marbled edges, per vol., $3.00.

This edition contains the Fourth Series—Tales from French history and is the only complete edition published in this country.

CHARLES DICKENS' COMPLETE WORKS. Author's Edition. 14 vols., with a portrait of the author on steel, and eight illustrations by F. O. C. Darley, Cruikshank, Fildes, Eytinge, and others, in each volume. 12mo. Cloth, extra, black and gold, per vol., $1.00; sheep, marbled edges, per vol., $1.50; half imt. Russia, marbled edges, per vol., $1.50: half calf, gilt, marbled edges, per vol., $2.75.

*Pickwick Papers.
*Oliver Twist, Pictures of Italy, and American Notes.
*Nicholas Nickleby.
Old Curiosity Shop, and Reprinted Pieces.
Barnaby Rudge, and Hard Times.
*Martin Chuzzlewit.
Dombey and Son.
*David Copperfield.
Christmas Books, Uncommercial Traveller, and Additional Christmas Stories.
Bleak House.
Little Dorrit.
Tale of Two Cities, and Great Expectations.
Our Mutual Friend.
Edwin Drood, Sketches, Master Humphrey's Clock, etc., etc.

Sold separately in cloth binding only.

*Also in Alta Edition, one illustration, 75 cents.

The same. Universe Edition. Printed on thin paper and containing one illustration to the volume. 14 vols., 12mo. Cloth, extra, black and gold, per vol., 75 cents.

The same. World Edition. 7 vols., thick 12mo., $12.25. (Sold in sets only.)

CHILD'S HISTORY OF ENGLAND. By CHARLES DICKENS. Popular 12mo. edition; from new electrotype plates. Large clear type. Beautifully illustrated with 8 engravings on wood. 12mo. Cloth, extra, black and gold, $1.00.

Alta Edition. One illustration, 75 cents.

"Dickens as a novelist and prose poet is to be classed in the front rank of the noble company to which he belongs. He has revived the novel of genuine practical life, as it existed in the works of Fielding, Smollett, and Goldsmith; but at the same time has given to his material an individual coloring and expression peculiarly his own. His characters, like those of his great exemplars, constitute a world of their own, whose truth to nature every reader instinctively recognizes in connection with their truth to darkness." —*E. P. Whipple.*

MACAULAY'S HISTORY OF ENGLAND. From the accession of James II. By THOMAS BABINGTON MACAULAY. With a steel portrait of the author. Printed from new electrotype plates from the last English Edition. Being by far the most correct edition in the American market. 5 volumes, 12mo. Cloth, extra, black and gold, per set, $5.00; sheep, marbled edges, per set, $7.50; half imitation Russia, $7.50; half calf, gilt, marbled edges, per set, $15.00.

Popular Edition. 5 vols., cloth, plain, $5.00.

8vo. Edition. 5 volumes in one, with portrait. Cloth, extra, black and gold, $3.00; sheep, marbled edges, $3.50.

MARTINEAU'S HISTORY OF ENGLAND. From the beginning of the 19th Century to the Crimean War. By HARRIET MARTINEAU. Complete in 4 vols., with full Index. Cloth, extra, black and gold, per set, $4.00; sheep, marbled edges, $6.00; half calf, gilt, marbled edges, $12.00.

HUME'S HISTORY OF ENGLAND. From the invasion of Julius Cæsar to the abdication of James II, 1688. By DAVID HUME. Standard Edition. With the author's last corrections and improvements; to which is prefixed a short account of his life, written by himself. With a portrait on steel. A new edition from entirely new stereotype plates. 5 vols., 12mo. Cloth, extra, black and gold, per set, $5.00; sheep, marbled edges, per set, $7.50; half imitation Russia, $7.50; half calf, gilt, marbled edges, per set, $15.00.

Popular Edition. 5 vols. Cloth, plain, $5.00.

GIBBON'S DECLINE AND FALL OF THE ROMAN EMPIRE. By EDWARD GIBBON. With Notes, by Rev. H. H. MILMAN. Standard Edition. To which is added a complete Index of the work. A new edition from entirely new stereotype plates. With portrait on steel. 5 vols., 12mo. Cloth, extra, black and gold, per set, $5.00; sheep, marbled edges, per set, $7.50; half imitation Russia, $7.50; half calf, gilt, marbled edges, per set, $15.00.

Popular Edition. 5 vols. Cloth, plain, $5.00.

ENGLAND, PICTURESQUE AND DESCRIPTIVE. By JOEL COOK, author of "A Holiday Tour in Europe," etc. With 487 finely engraved illustrations, descriptive of the most famous and attractive places, as well as of the historic scenes and rural life of England and Wales. With Mr. Cook's admirable descriptions of the places and the country, and the splendid illustrations, this is the most valuable and attractive book of the season, and the sale will doubtless be very large. 4to. Cloth, extra, gilt side and edges, $7.50; half calf, gilt, marbled edges, $10.00; half morocco, full gilt edges, $10.00; full Turkey morocco, gilt edges, $15.00; tree calf, gilt edges, $18.00.

This work, which is prepared in elegant style, and profusely illustrated, is a comprehensive description of England and Wales, arranged in convenient form for the tourist, and at the same time providing an illustrated guide-book to a country which Americans always view with interest. There are few satisfactory works about this land which is so generously gifted by Nature and so full of memorials of the past. Such books as there are, either cover a few counties or are devoted to special localities, or are merely guide-books. The present work is believed to be the first attempt to give in attractive form a description of the stately homes, renowned castles, ivy-clad ruins of abbeys, churches, and ancient fortresses, delicious scenery, rock-bound coasts, and celebrated places of England and Wales. It is written by an author fully competent from travel and reading, and in position to properly describe his very interesting subject; and the artist's pencil has been called into requisition to graphically illustrate its well-written pages. There are 487 illustrations, prepared in the highest style of the engraver's art, while the book itself is one of the most attractive ever presented to the American public.

Its method of construction is systematic, following the most convenient routes taken by tourists, and the letter-press includes enough of the history and legend of each of the places described to make the story highly interesting. Its pages fairly overflow with picture and description, telling of everything attractive that is presented by England and Wales. Executed in the highest style of the printer's and engraver's art, "England, Picturesque and Descriptive," is one of the best American books of the year.

HISTORY OF THE CIVIL WAR IN AMERICA. By the COMTE DE PARIS. With Maps faithfully Engraved from the Originals, and Printed in Three Colors. 8vo. Cloth, per volume $3.50; red cloth, extra, Roxburgh style, uncut edges, $3.50; sheep, library style, $4.50; half Turkey morocco, $6.00. Vols I, II, and III now ready.

The third volume embraces, without abridgment, the fifth and sixth volumes of the French edition, and covers one of the most interesting as well as the most anxious periods of the war, describing the operations of the Army of the Potomac in the East, and the Army of the Cumberland and Tennessee in the West.

It contains full accounts of the battle of Chancellorsville, the attack of the monitors on Fort Sumter, the sieges and fall of Vicksburg and Port Hudson; the battles of Port Gibson and Champion's Hill, and the fullest and most authentic account of the battle of Gettysburg ever written.

"The head of the Orleans family has put pen to paper with excellent result. . . . . Our present impression is that it will form by far the best history of the American war."—*Athenæum, London.*

"We advise all Americans to read it carefully, and judge for themselves if 'the future historian of our war,' of whom we have heard so much, be not already arrived in the Comte de Paris."—*Nation, New York.*

"This is incomparably the best account of our great second revolution that has yet been even attempted. It is so calm, so dispassionate, so accurate in detail, and at the same time so philosophical in general, that its reader counts confidently on finding the complete work thoroughly satisfactory."—*Evening Bulletin, Philadelphia.*

"The work expresses the calm, deliberate judgment of an experienced military observer and a highly intelligent man. Many of its statements will excite discussion, but we much mistake if it does not take high and permanent rank among the standard histories of the civil war. Indeed that place has been assigned it by the most competent critics both of this country and abroad."—*Times, Cincinnati.*

"Messrs. Porter & Coates, of Philadelphia, will publish in a few days the authorized translation of the new volume of the Comte de Paris' History of Our Civil War. The two volumes in French—the fifth and sixth—are bound together in the translation in one volume. Our readers already know, through a table of contents of these volumes, published in the cable columns of the *Herald*, the period covered by this new installment of a work remarkable in several ways. It includes the most important and decisive period of the war, and the two great campaigns of Gettysburg and Vicksburg.

"The great civil war has had no better, no abler historian than the French prince who, emulating the example of Lafayette, took part in this new struggle for freedom, and who now writes of events, in many of which he participated, as an accomplished officer, and one who, by his independent position, his high character and eminent talents, was placed in circumstances and relations which gave him almost unequalled opportunities to gain correct information and form impartial judgments.

"The new installment of a work which has already become a classic will be read with increased interest by Americans because of the importance of the period it covers and the stirring events it describes. In advance of a careful review we present to-day some extracts from the advance sheets sent us by Messrs. Porter & Coates, which will give our readers a foretaste of chapters which bring back to memory so many half-forgotten and not a few hitherto unvalued details of a time which Americans of this generation at least cannot read of without a fresh thrill of excitement."

HALF-HOURS WITH THE BEST AUTHORS. With short Biographical and Critical Notes. By CHARLES KNIGHT.

New Household Edition. With six portraits on steel. 3 vols., thick 12mo. Cloth, extra, black and gold, per set, $4.50; half imt. Russia, marbled edges, $6.00; half calf, gilt, marbled edges, $12.00.

Library Edition. Printed on fine laid and tinted paper. With twenty-four portraits on steel. 6 vols., 12mo. Cloth, extra, per set, $7.50; half calf, gilt, marbled edges, per set, $18.00; half Russia, gilt top, $21.00; full French morocco, limp, per set, $12.00; full smooth Russia, limp, round corners, in Russia case, per set, $25.00; full seal grained Russia, limp, round corners, in Russia case to match, $25.00.

The excellent idea of the editor of these choice volumes has been most admirably carried out, as will be seen by the list of authors upon all subjects. Selecting some choice passages of the best standard authors, each of sufficient length to occupy half an hour in its perusal, there is here food for thought for every day in the year: so that if the purchaser will devote but one-half hour each day to its appropriate selection he will read through these six volumes in one year, and in such a leisurely manner that the noblest thoughts of many of the greatest minds will be firmly in his mind forever. For every Sunday there is a suitable selection from some of the most eminent writers in sacred literature. We venture to say if the editor's idea is carried out the reader will possess more and better knowledge of the English classics at the end of the year than he would by five years of desultory reading.

They can be commenced at any day in the year. The variety of reading is so great that no one will ever tire of these volumes. It is a library in itself.

THE POETRY OF OTHER LANDS. A Collection of Translations into English Verse of the Poetry of Other Languages, Ancient and Modern. Compiled by N. CLEMMONS HUNT. Containing translations from the Greek, Latin, Persian, Arabian, Japanese, Turkish, Servian, Russian, Bohemian, Polish, Dutch, German, Italian, French, Spanish, and Portuguese languages. 12mo. Cloth, extra, gilt edges, $2.50; half calf, gilt, marbled edges, $4.00; Turkey morocco, gilt edges, $6.00.

"Another of the publications of Porter & Coates, called 'The Poetry of Other Lands,' compiled by N. Clemmons Hunt, we most warmly commend. It is one of the best collections we have seen, containing many exquisite poems and fragments of verse which have not before been put into book form in English words. We find many of the old favorites, which appear in every well-selected collection of sonnets and songs, and we miss others, which seem a necessity to complete the bouquet of grasses and flowers, some of which, from time to time, we hope to republish in the 'Courier.'"—*Cincinnati Courier.*

"A book of rare excellence, because it gives a collection of choice gems in many languages not available to the general lover of poetry. It contains translations from the Greek, Latin, Persian, Arabian, Japanese, Turkish, Servian, Russian, Bohemian, Polish, Dutch, German, Italian, French, Spanish, and Portuguese languages. The book will be an admirable companion volume to any one of the collections of English poetry that are now published. With the full index of authors immediately preceding the collection, and the arrangement of the poems under headings, the reader will find it convenient for reference. It is a gift that will be more valued by very many than some of the transitory ones at these holiday times."—*Philadelphia Methodist.*

THE FIRESIDE ENCYCLOPÆDIA OF POETRY. Edited by HENRY T. COATES. This is the latest, and beyond doubt the best collection of poetry published. Printed on fine paper and illustrated with thirteen steel engravings and fifteen title pages, containing portraits of prominent American poets and fac-similes of their handwriting, made expressly for this book. 8vo. Cloth, extra, black and gold, gilt edges, $5.00; half calf, gilt, marbled edges, $7.50; half morocco, full gilt edges, $7.50; full Turkey morocco, gilt edges, $10.00; tree calf, gilt edges, $12.00; plush, padded side, nickel lettering, $14.00.

"The editor shows a wide acquaintance with the most precious treasures of English verse, and has gathered the most admirable specimens of their ample wealth. Many pieces which have been passed by in previous collections hold a place of honor in the present volume, and will be heartily welcomed by the lovers of poetry as a delightful addition to their sources of enjoyment. It is a volume rich in solace, in entertainment, in inspiration, of which the possession may well be coveted by every lover of poetry. The pictorial illustrations of the work are in keeping with its poetical contents, and the beauty of the typographical execution entitles it to a place among the choicest ornaments of the library."—*New York Tribune.*

"Lovers of good poetry will find this one of the richest collections ever made. All the best singers in our language are represented, and the selections are generally those which reveal their highest qualities. . . . . The lights and shades, the finer play of thought and imagination belonging to individual authors, are brought out in this way (by the arrangement of poems under subject-headings) as they would not be under any other system. . . . . We are deeply impressed with the keen appreciation of poetical worth, and also with the good taste manifested by the compiler."—*Churchman.*

"Cyclopædias of poetry are numerous, but for sterling value of its contents for the library, or as a book of reference, no work of the kind will compare with this admirable volume of Mr. Coates. It takes the gems from many volumes, culling with rare skill and judgment."—*Chicago Inter-Ocean.*

THE CHILDREN'S BOOK OF POETRY. Compiled by HENRY T. COATES. Containing over 500 poems carefully selected from the works of the best and most popular writers for children; with nearly 200 illustrations. The most complete collection of poetry for children ever published. 4to. Cloth, extra, black and gold, gilt side and edges, $3.00; full Turkey morocco, gilt edges, $7.50.

"This seems to us the best book of poetry for children in existence. We have examined many other collections, but we cannot name another that deserves to be compared with this admirable compilation."—*Worcester Spy.*

"The special value of the book lies in the fact that it nearly or quite covers the entire field. There is not a great deal of good poetry which has been written for children that cannot be found in this book. The collection is particularly strong in ballads and tales, which are apt to interest children more than poems of other kinds; and Mr. Coates has shown good judgment in supplementing this department with some of the best poems of that class that have been written for grown people. A surer method of forming the taste of children for good and pure literature than by reading to them from any portion of this book can hardly be imagined. The volume is richly illustrated and beautifully bound."—*Philadelphia Evening Bulletin.*

"A more excellent volume cannot be found. We have found within the covers of this handsome volume, and upon its fair pages, many of the most exquisite poems which our language contains. It must become a standard volume, and can never grow old or obsolete."—*Episcopal Recorder.*

THE COMPLETE WORKS OF THOS. HOOD. With engravings on steel. 4 vols., 12mo., tinted paper. Poetical Works; Up the Rhine; Miscellanies and Hood's Own; Whimsicalities, Whims, and Oddities. Cloth, extra, black and gold, $6.00; red cloth, paper label, gilt top, uncut edges, $6.00; half calf, gilt, marbled edges, $14.00; half Russia, gilt top, $18.00.

Hood's verse, whether serious or comic—whether serene like a cloudless autumn evening or sparkling with puns like a frosty January midnight with stars—was ever pregnant with materials for the thought. Like every author distinguished for true comic humor, there was a deep vein of melancholy pathos running through his mirth, and even when his sun shone brightly its light seemed often reflected as if only over the rim of a cloud.

Well may we say, in the words of Tennyson, "Would he could have stayed with us." for never could it be more truly recorded of any one—in the words of Hamlet characterizing Yorick—that "he was a fellow of infinite jest, of most excellent fancy." D. M. MOIR.

THE ILIAD OF HOMER RENDERED INTO ENGLISH BLANK VERSE. By EDWARD, EARL OF DERBY. From the latest London edition, with all the author's last revisions and corrections, and with a Biographical Sketch of Lord Derby, by R. SHELTON MACKENZIE, D.C.L. With twelve steel engravings from Flaxman's celebrated designs. 2 vols., 12mo. Cloth, extra, bev. boards, gilt top, $3.50; half calf, gilt, marbled edges, $7.00; half Turkey morocco, gilt top, $7.00.

The same. Popular edition. Two vols. in one. 12mo. Cloth, extra, $1.50.

"It must equally be considered a splendid performance; and for the present we have no hesitation in saying that it is by far the best representation of Homer's Iliad in the English language."—*London Times.*

"The merits of Lord Derby's translation may be summed up in one word, it is eminently attractive; it is instinct with life; it may be read with fervent interest; it is immeasurably nearer than Pope to the text of the original. . . . . Lord Derby has given a version far more closely allied to the original, and superior to any that has yet been attempted in the blank verse of our language."—*Edinburg Review.*

THE WORKS OF FLAVIUS JOSEPHUS. Comprising the Antiquities of the Jews; a History of the Jewish Wars, and a Life of Flavius Josephus, written by himself. Translated from the original Greek, by WILLIAM WHISTON, A.M. Together with numerous explanatory Notes and seven Dissertations concerning Jesus Christ, John the Baptist, James the Just, God's command to Abraham, etc., with an Introductory Essay by Rev. H. STEBBING, D.D. 8vo. Cloth, extra, black and gold, plain edges, $3.00; cloth, red, black and gold, gilt edges, $4.50; sheep, marbled edges, $3.50; Turkey morocco, gilt edges, $8.00.

This is the largest type one volume edition published.

THE ANCIENT HISTORY OF THE EGYPTIANS, CARTHAGINIANS, ASSYRIANS, BABYLONIANS, MEDES AND PERSIANS, GRECIANS AND MACEDONIANS Including a History of the Arts and Sciences of the Ancients. By CHARLES ROLLIN. With a Life of the Author, by JAMES BELL. 2 vols., royal 8vo. Sheep, marbled edges, per set, $6.00.

COOKERY FROM EXPERIENCE. A Practical Guide for Housekeepers in the Preparation of Every-day Meals, containing more than One Thousand Domestic Recipes, mostly tested by Personal Experience, with Suggestions for Meals, Lists of Meats and Vegetables in Season, etc. By Mrs. SARA T. PAUL. 12mo. Cloth, extra, black and gold, $1.50.

Interleaved Edition. Cloth, extra, black and gold, $1.75.

THE COMPARATIVE EDITION OF THE NEW TESTAMENT. Both Versions in One Book.

The proof readings of our Comparative Edition have been gone over by so many competent proof readers, that we believe the text is absolutely correct.

Large 12mo., 700 pp. Cloth, extra, plain edges, $1.50; cloth, extra, bevelled boards and carmine edges, $1.75; imitation panelled calf, yellow edges, $2.00; arabesque, gilt edges, $2.50; French morocco, limp, gilt edges, $4.00; Turkey morocco, limp, gilt edges, $6.00.

The Comparative New Testament has been published by Porter & Coates. In parallel columns on each page are given the old and new versions of the Testament, divided also as far as practicable into comparative verses, so that it is almost impossible for the slightest new word to escape the notice of either the ordinary reader or the analytical student. It is decidedly the best edition yet published of the most interest-exciting literary production of the day. No more convenient form for comparison could be devised either for economizing time or labor. Another feature is the foot-notes, and there is also given in an appendix the various words and expressions preferred by the American members of the Revising Commission. The work is handsomely printed on excellent paper with clear, legible type. It contains nearly 700 pages.

THE COUNT OF MONTE CRISTO. By ALEXANDRE DUMAS. Complete in one volume, with two illustrations by George G. White. 12mo. Cloth, extra, black and gold, $1.25.

THE THREE GUARDSMEN. By ALEXANDRE DUMAS. Complete in one volume, with two illustrations by George G. White. 12mo. Cloth, extra, black and gold, $1.25.

There is a magic influence in his pen, a magnetic attraction in his descriptions, a fertility in his literary resources which are characteristic of Dumas alone, and the seal of the master of light literature is set upon all his works. Even when not strictly historical, his romances give an insight into the habits and modes of thought and action of the people of the time described, which are not offered in any other author's productions.

THE LAST DAYS OF POMPEII. By Sir EDWARD BULWER LYTTON, Bart. Illustrated. 12mo. Cloth, extra, black and gold, $1.00. Alta edition, one illustration, 75 cts.

JANE EYRE. By CHARLOTTE BRONTÉ (Currer Bell). New Library Edition. With five illustrations by E. M. WIMPERIS. 12mo. Cloth, extra, black and gold, $1.00.

SHIRLEY. By CHARLOTTE BRONTÉ (Currer Bell). New Library Edition. With five illustrations by E. M. WIMPERIS. 12mo. Cloth, extra, black and gold, $1.00.

VILLETTE. By CHARLOTTE BRONTÉ (Currer Bell). New Library Edition. With five illustrations by E. M. WIMPERIS. 12mo. Cloth, extra, black and gold, $1.00.

THE PROFESSOR, EMMA and POEMS. By CHARLOTTE BRONTÉ (Currer Bell). New Library Edition. With five illustrations by E. M. WIMPERIS. 12mo. Cloth, extra, black and gold, $1.00.

Cloth, extra, black and gold, per set, $4.00; red cloth, paper label, gilt top, uncut edges, per set, $5.00; half calf, gilt, per set, $12.00. The four volumes forming the complete works of Charlotte Bronté (Currer Bell).

The wondrous power of Currer Bell's stories consists in their fiery insight into the human heart, their merciless dissection of passion, and their stern analysis of character and motive. The style of these productions possesses incredible force, sometimes almost grim in its bare severity, then relapsing into passages of melting pathos—always direct, natural, and effective in its unpretending strength. They exhibit the identity which always belongs to works of genius by the same author, though without the slightest approach to monotony. The characters portrayed by Currer Bell all have a strongly marked individuality. Once brought before the imagination, they haunt the memory like a strange dream. The sinewy, muscular strength of her writings guarantees their permanent duration, and thus far they have lost nothing of their intensity of interest since the period of their composition.

CAPTAIN JACK THE SCOUT; or, The Indian Wars about Old Fort Duquesne. An Historical Novel, with copious notes. By CHARLES MCKNIGHT. Illustrated with eight engravings. 12mo. Cloth, extra, black and gold, $1.50.

A work of such rare merit and thrilling interest as to have been republished both in England and Germany. This genuine American historical work has been received with extraordinary popular favor, and has "won golden opinions from all sorts of people" for its freshness, its forest life, and its fidelity to truth. In many instances it even corrects History and uses the drapery of fiction simply to enliven and illustrate the fact.

It is a universal favorite with both sexes, and with all ages and conditions, and is not only proving a marked and notable success in this country, but has been eagerly taken up abroad and republished in London, England, and issued in two volumes in the far-famed "Tauchnetz Edition" of Leipsic, Germany.

ORANGE BLOSSOMS, FRESH AND FADED. By T. S. ARTHUR. Illustrated. 12mo. Cloth, extra, black and gold, $1.50.

"Orange Blossoms" contains a number of short stories of society. Like all of Mr. Arthur's works, it has a special moral purpose, and is especially addressed to the young who have just entered the marital experience, whom it pleasantly warns against those social and moral pitfalls into which they may almost innocently plunge.

THE BAR ROOMS AT BRANTLEY; or, The Great Hotel Speculation. By T. S. ARTHUR. Illustrated. 12mo. Cloth, extra, black and gold, $1.50.

"One of the best temperance stories recently issued."—*N. Y. Commercial Advertiser.*

"Although it is in the form of a novel, its truthful delineation of characters is such that in every village in the land you meet the broken manhood it pictures upon the streets, and look upon sad, tear-dimmed eyes of women and children. The characters are not overdrawn, but are as truthful as an artist's pencil could make them."—*Inter-Ocean, Chicago.*

EMMA. By JANE AUSTEN. Illustrated. 12mo. Cloth, extra, $1.25.

MANSFIELD PARK. By JANE AUSTEN. Illustrated. 12mo. Cloth, extra, $1.25.

PRIDE AND PREJUDICE; and Northanger Abbey. By JANE AUSTEN. Illustrated. 12mo. Cloth, extra, $1.25.

SENSE AND SENSIBILITY; and Persuasion. By JANE AUSTEN. Illustrated. 12mo. Cloth, extra, $1.25.

The four volumes, forming the complete works of Jane Austen, in a neat box: Cloth, extra, per set, $5.00; red cloth, paper label, gilt top, uncut edges, $5.00; half calf, gilt, per set, $12.00.

"Jane Austen, a woman of whom England is justly proud. In her novels she has given us a multitude of characters, all, in a certain sense, commonplace, all such as we meet every day. Yet they are all as perfectly discriminated from each other as if they were the most eccentric of human beings. . . . . And almost all this is done by touches so delicate that they elude analysis, that they defy the powers of description, and that we know them to exist only by the general effect to which they have contributed."—*Macaulay's Essays.*

ART AT HOME. Containing in one volume House Decoration, by RHODA and AGNES GARRETT; Plea for Art in the House, by W. J. LOFTIE; Music, by JOHN HULLAH; and Dress, by Mrs. OLIPHANT. 12mo. Cloth, extra, black and gold, $1.50.

TOM BROWN'S SCHOOL DAYS AT RUGBY. By THOMAS HUGHES. New Edition, large clear type. With 36 illustrations after Caldecott and others. 12mo., 400 pp. Cloth, extra, black and gold, $1.25; half calf, gilt, $2.75.
Alta Edition. One illustration, 75 cents.

"It is difficult to estimate the amount of good which may be done by 'Tom Brown's School Days.' It gives, in the main, a most faithful and interesting picture of our public schools, the most English institutions of England, and which educate the best and most powerful elements in our upper classes. But it is more than this; it is an attempt, a very noble and successful attempt, to Christianize the society of our youth, through the only practicable channel—hearty and brotherly sympathy with their feelings; a book, in short, which a father might well wish to see in the hands of his son."—*London Times.*

TOM BROWN AT OXFORD. By THOMAS HUGHES. Illustrated. 12mo. Cloth, extra, black and gold, $1.50; half calf, gilt, $3.00.

"Fairly entitled to the rank and dignity of an English classic. Plot, style and truthfulness are of the soundest British character. Racy, idiomatic, mirror-like, always interesting, suggesting thought on the knottiest social and religious questions, now deeply moving by its unconscious pathos, and anon inspiring uproarious laughter, it is a work the world will not willingly let die."—*N. Y. Christian Advocate.*

SENSIBLE ETIQUETTE OF THE BEST SOCIETY. By Mrs. H. O. WARD. Customs, manners, morals, and home culture, with suggestions how to word notes and letters of invitations, acceptances, and regrets, and general instructions as to calls, rules for watering places, lunches, kettle drums, dinners, receptions, weddings, parties, dress, toilet and manners, salutations, introductions, social reforms, etc., etc. Bound in cloth, with gilt edge, and sent by mail, postage paid, on receipt of $2.00.

LADIES' AND GENTLEMEN'S ETIQUETTE: A Complete Manual of the Manners and Dress of American Society. Containing forms of Letters, Invitations, Acceptances, and Regrets. With a copious index. By E. B. DUFFEY. 12mo. Cloth, extra, black and gold, $1.50.

"It is peculiarly an American book, especially adapted to our people, and its greatest beauty is found in the fact that in every line and precept it inculcates the principles of true politeness, instead of those formal rules that serve only to gild the surface without affecting the substance. It is admirably written, the style being clear, terse, and forcible."—*St. Louis Times.*

THE UNDERGROUND CITY; or, The Child of the Cavern. By JULES VERNE. Translated from the French by W. H. KINGSTON. With 43 illustrations. Standard Edition. 12mo. Cloth, extra, black and gold, $1.50.

AROUND THE WORLD IN EIGHTY DAYS. By JULES VERNE. Translated by GEO. M. TOWLE. With 12 full-page illustrations. 12mo. Cloth, extra, black and gold, $1.25.

AT THE NORTH POLE; or, The Voyages and Adventures of Captain Hatteras. By JULES VERNE. With 130 illustrations by RIOU. Standard Edition. 12mo. Cloth, extra, black and gold, $1.25.

THE DESERT OF ICE; or, The Further Adventures of Captain Hatteras. By JULES VERNE. With 126 illustrations by RIOU. Standard Edition. 12mo. Cloth, extra, black and gold, $1.25.

TWENTY THOUSAND LEAGUES UNDER THE SEAS; or, The Marvellous and Exciting Adventures of Pierre Aronnax, Conseil his servant, and Ned Land, a Canadian Harpooner. By JULES VERNE. Standard Edition. Illustrated. 12mo. Cloth, extra, black and gold, $1.25.

THE WRECK OF THE CHANCELLOR, Diary of J. R. Kazallon, Passenger, and Martin Paz. By JULES VERNE. Translated from the French by ELLEN FREWER. With 10 illustrations. Standard Edition. 12mo. Cloth, extra, black and gold, $1.25.

Jules Verne is so well known that the mere announcement of anything from his pen is sufficient to create a demand for it. One of his chief merits is the wonderful art with which he lays under contribution every branch of science and natural history, while he vividly describes with minute exactness all parts of the world and its inhabitants.

THE INGOLDSBY LEGENDS; or, Mirth and Marvels. By RICHARD HARRIS BARHAM (Thomas Ingoldsby, Esq.). New edition, printed from entirely new stereotype plates. Illustrated. 12mo. Cloth, extra, black and gold, $1.50; half calf, gilt, marbled edges, $3.00.

"Of his poetical powers it is not too much to say that, for originality of design and diction, for grand illustration and musical verse, they are not surpassed in the English language. The Witches' Frolic is second only to Tam O'Shanter. But why recapitulate the titles of either prose or verse—since they have been confessed by every judgment to be singularly rich in classic allusion and modern illustration. From the days of Hudibras to our time the drollery invested in rhymes has never been so amply or felicitously exemplified."—*Bentley's Miscellany.*

TEN THOUSAND A YEAR. By SAMUEL C. WARREN, author of "The Diary of a London Physician." A new edition, carefully revised, with three illustrations by GEORGE G. WHITE. 12mo. Cloth, extra, black and gold, $1 50.

"Mr. Warren has taken a lasting place among the imaginative writers of this period of English history. He possesses, in a remarkable manner, the tenderness of heart and vividness of feeling, as well as powers of description, which are essential to the delineation of the pathetic, and which, when existing in the degree in which he enjoys them, fill his pages with scenes which can never be forgotten."—*Sir Archibald Alison.*

THOMPSON'S POLITICAL ECONOMY; With Especial Reference to the Industrial History of Nations. By Prof. R. E. THOMPSON, of the University of Pennsylvania. 12mo. Cloth, extra, $1.50.

This book possesses an especial interest at the present moment. The questions of Free Trade and Protection are before the country more directly than at any earlier period of our history. As a rule the works and text-books used in our American colleges are either of English origin or teach Doctrines of a political economy which, as Walter Bagehot says, was made for England. Prof. Thompson belongs to the Nationalist School of Economists, to which Alexander Hamilton, Tench Coxe, Henry Clay, Matthew Carey, and his greater son, Henry C. Carey, Stephen Colwell, and James Abram Garfield were adherents. He believes in that policy of Protection to American industry which has had the sanction of every great American statesman, not excepting Thomas Jefferson and John C. Calhoun. He makes his appeal to history in defence of that policy, showing that wherever a weaker or less advanced country has practiced Free Trade with one more powerful or richer, the former has lost its industries as well as its money, and has become economically dependent on the latter. Those who wish to learn what is the real source of Irish poverty and discontent will find it here stated fully.

The method of the book is historical. It is therefore no series of dry and abstract reasonings, such as repel readers from books of this class. The writer does not ride the *a priori* nag, and say "this must be so," and "that must be conceded." He shows what has been true, and seeks to elicit the laws of the science from the experience of the world. The book overflows with facts told in an interesting manner.

THE ENGLISH PEOPLE IN ITS THREE HOMES, and the Practical Bearings of general European History. By EDWARD A. FREEMAN, LL.D., Author of the "Norman Conquest of England." 12mo. Cloth, extra, $1.75.

www.ingramcontent.com/pod-product-compliance
Lightning Source LLC
LaVergne TN
LVHW010228110826
845151LV00004B/1225

* 9 7 8 1 4 2 5 5 2 5 6 5 1 *